RECORDING A
KILL

JIM HENNINGER

RECORDING A KILL

TATE PUBLISHING
AND ENTERPRISES, LLC

Recording A Kill
Copyright © 2014 by Jim Henninger. All rights reserved.

This novel is a work of fiction. Names, descriptions, entities, and incidents included in the story are products of the author's imagination. Any resemblance to actual persons, events, and entities is entirely coincidental.

The opinions expressed by the author are not necessarily those of Tate Publishing, LLC.

Published by Tate Publishing & Enterprises, LLC
127 E. Trade Center Terrace | Mustang, Oklahoma 73064 USA
1.888.361.9473 | www.tatepublishing.com

Tate Publishing is committed to excellence in the publishing industry. The company reflects the philosophy established by the founders, based on Psalm 68:11,
"The Lord gave the word and great was the company of those who published it."

Published in the United States of America

ISBN: 978-1-63122-167-5
1. Fiction / Thrillers / Suspense
2. Fiction / Thrillers / General
14.03.10

MONDAY

It's shortly after midnight, and I'm blasting through the thick dark woods. There are branches, stickers, and all types of resistant foliage thrashing at me. That monster is after me, and I'm not gonna let him catch me, or worse, shoot me, if I can help it. I feel a strange balance between adrenaline and abject terror in my body.

Every few seconds, I beg God to help me. I look for signs that he's decided to spare me, but all I'm aware of is the ever-nearing sounds of my pursuer. My stomach is clenching and feels like a bottomless cramp. I'm giving it everything I've got to get away from this situation or die trying. I'm beginning to accept the likelihood that the latter is probably the more likely outcome at this point.

I'm not sure how long I've been running through these thick forlorn woods. Every once in a while, I see a light and try to run toward it. I hope, beyond hope, that it's a porch light or maybe a security light. Unfortunately, it seems like an insurmountable obstacle, such as a sudden appearing drop-off to a creek or a small waterfall, repeatedly forces me to change course. And every time something gets in my way and I have to change direction, I lose track of the light I was honing in on.

I already tried resting by hiding in some bushes when I was near exhaustion. Unfortunately, the murderer came directly at me a few minutes later, and when he was about twenty feet away, I broke cover and resumed my flight. He fired a shot at me, which tested my bladder control. The bullet seemed to pass only inches over my head. I hurriedly reached the conclusion that stopping to hide, for any reason, was no longer an option.

My eyes are stinging with sweat, and I can taste blood dripping into my mouth from numerous cuts on my forehead and face. My cell phone, still in my pants pocket, is soaking wet. When I tried to use it in the bushes earlier, it wouldn't even power up, much less work. Thank goodness I'm wearing dark clothes and have black greasepaint on my face and head. I experience a brief flash of shame for the reason I'm attired in this fashion.

I'm not sure if I've been running for twenty minutes or two hours, and at this point, I'm no longer worried about making noise as my nightmare continues. All of a sudden, I fly out of a line of thick thorny shrubs and land about three feet outward into a shallow and muddy pond. Glancing to my right, I see the outline of a two-story house. Since it's late, the windows are dark.

I'm about to scream at the top of my lungs when the guy chasing me appears on the opposite side of the pond about two hundred feet away. I stare and see his gleaming white teeth and what appears to be a demonic smile. I quickly turn away and start extricating myself from the muddy, soggy bottom of the pond. In the process, I lose both of my tennis shoes to the mucky mess.

Scrambling toward the edge of the pond and what I hope will be help from a homeowner, I start stepping on rocks and sharp sticks. I feel something pierce the skin on the bottom of my left foot, but I grimace and keep climbing upward toward the house. It's super dark, but there's some faint moonlight shining through the trees. This allows me to quickly navigate to the side of the house. I think that if I can get this house between me and my pursuer, I can pound on the walls and scream for help. Unfortunately, when I get closer, I realize the house is under construction. *Oh my God,* I think to myself.

Looking around for any signs of other houses, all I see is a dark cul-de-sac surrounded by trees. I make a quick decision that running with no shoes on asphalt is preferable to tearing up my feet in the woods. I'm no more than forty feet down the road, lungs burning and gasping for breath, when I hear the guy chasing me scream, "I've got you now, you bastard! Stop or I'll shoot!"

He then fires a shot about a foot to my left into the asphalt. I feel some pieces of the road strike my pant leg. He fires a second shot close to my right. Both shots were deafening. He has my attention. I skid to a halt, and simultaneously, a flood of tears come to my eyes, blinding me. I think about raising my hands in surrender, but I don't have the strength to do it.

Slowly, I pivot and decide my time on this earth is quickly coming to an end. With that evil grin still framing his face, my pursuer slowly walks toward me, keeping the gun pointed directly at my chest. As he closes the gap between us, I pass out.

CHAPTER 2

MONDAY: THREE WEEKS EARLIER

It's a clear and bright July Monday morning in Alpharetta, Georgia, and, all things considered, I'm a lucky man. I have two well-adjusted, successful adult children who live in Texas and Illinois. My daughter, divorced and working on her PhD at Texas Tech while raising two border collies, is thirty-three years old and small of stature.

My slightly younger son is 6'2", weighs north of 230 pounds, and sells asphalt road contracts to municipalities. He is married to a slightly built firebrand of a girl who is an artist. Unfortunately, the love of my life for thirty-six years died of a progressive lung disease about two years ago. No one in her immediate family had this problem, but Linda gave us all a lesson in being strong and living her life to the fullest until the disease finally won out.

As for me, Kevin Harrington, I'm fifty-six years old, and like many of my middle-aged contemporaries, I carry a little too much weight and not quite enough hair. I work out of my home as a field representative for Disability Protection Group (DPG). A medium sized carrier on the New York Stock Exchange, DPG offers a variety of disability products to its customers, including individual disability insurance policies.

Simply put, my job is to conduct face-to-face interviews, known in the industry as field visits, with customers filing new or ongoing disability claims. DPG's disability claims office is located in Houston, Texas. I'm required to go into the Houston office twice a year to meet with the claim processors and my boss. The rest of the time, I travel across eight states interviewing claimants, their employers, their coworkers, and others with knowledge of their medical or vocational background.

My Mondays and Fridays are typically spent in my home office scheduling appointments, making travel arrangements, and dictating field reports to send to Houston. I see about 140 people a year in the southeastern United States from Raleigh, North Carolina, to New Orleans, Louisiana.

Today, I check my e-mail, and find I have three new referrals to schedule appointments with over the next few weeks. One is a lady who lives south of Birmingham, Alabama, named Ms. Gayle Wade. The claim file will follow the referral sheet, but it appears she fell in a convenience store and injured her back. I reach her on the phone and make a routine appointment with her for a week from tomorrow. Little do I know that this visit will be far from the norm and end up turning my world upside down.

MONDAY: TWO WEEKS EARLIER

Today is one of my usual two weekdays in my home office, and I'm busy. I dictate reports detailing the three field interviews I conducted in Louisiana during a two-day trip last week. I check my flight arrangements for this week, which consists of a two-day trip to Raleigh, North Carolina, to interview two claimants on Thursday and Friday.

Because it's only about 110 miles from my house to the home of Ms. Wade in Helena, Alabama, I plan to be a good company soldier and rent a car at the Atlanta airport. This adheres to the stated corporate policy in which we are encouraged to rent cars instead of driving our own vehicles and turning in for mileage reimbursement. Actually, I prefer this arrangement so I can avoid putting more miles on my five-year-old Chevy TrailBlazer.

I sit at my in-home work station and finish dictating a report as well as scheduling appointments with referrals in

South Carolina and Tennessee for the next few weeks. I am lucky. I reach some claimants, make some appointments, and make the appropriate air travel arrangements. At about 4:00 p.m., I have some time to review Ms. Wade's claim, which I received a copy of late last week via a Federal Express shipment from the claim office.

As I read through it, I realize that this is not a clear-cut claim scenario as is sometimes the case. By this, I mean she didn't suffer a fracture or have a knee replacement, incidents which are almost disabling on their face value. She is filing for a fall in a convenience store in which she claims she injured her back. She indicates the fall happened about ten weeks ago at a Circle K Store in South Birmingham, and she suffered an undisclosed spinal injury.

I know, without asking, that the claim department has already begun their adjudication process to include ordering the records from all of Ms. Wade's medical providers. I notice that she lists two treating physicians—an orthopedic surgeon who she reported treated her about a week after her fall and a family practitioner who she said she hasn't seen for about four months.

I make notations to help me conduct the interview tomorrow and include a reminder to ask what the surgeon told her and if she was referred to him for this evaluation. I note that she indicates she is the Chief Financial Officer (CFO) for MB Construction Company. I Google this company and nothing turns up, which seems unusual but may be explainable. I make a note to ask about her employer not having any apparent Internet presence.

I answer a couple of calls from the claim office while I'm reviewing the file and request one of the callers to forward me to the claim examiner in charge of Ms. Wade's claim. She tells me that she has just begun requesting medical records from the two doctors identified in the claim forms and knows nothing other than what is in the information she forwarded to me last week. She said she is not aware of anything strange about the claimant's employer, although she hasn't received a completed employer's statement from the construction company regarding Ms. Wade. I thank her and end the call.

It's approaching 6:00 p.m., and I feel confident I have gleaned all of the facts I can from reviewing the available information. I put my PC, my notes, and all of the related paperwork concerning Ms. Wade into my computer bag in preparation to leave in the morning. Ms. Wade and I agreed to meet at her house at noon tomorrow, and I have to allow sufficient time to drive to the airport and pick up a rental car.

As a widower of nearly two years, I have refused to hone my cooking skills, which are limited to making breakfast and operating a toaster. Accordingly, I open the freezer and select one of several frozen meals I purchased from the Schwan's man. He delivers food to me every other Wednesday night via his large refrigerated truck. If I know I'm not going to be home, I leave my dog sitter instructions concerning what to buy. I'm never out of pizza, frozen steaks, or dog treats, although the treats come from the grocery store. It's nearly 7:30 p.m., and the first bite is on the way to my open mouth when the doorbell rings. I glance out the front window and notice the single older woman from down the street. Without trying to sound stuck-up, she has an obvious crush on me and occasionally brings me something to eat or slowly walks her dog by my house. My beagle and collie are greeting her with a chorus of barks and howls. I brace myself and open the door. I tell her my dinner is getting cold but graciously accept her culinary offering.

After she turns to leave, not bothering to hide the disappointed look on her face, I take her paper plate of something that resembles recycled bean dip and throw it into the kitchen trash can. I then sit down to eat my not-so-healthy serving of beef tips and mashed potatoes. My mind drifts to my meeting with Ms. Wade tomorrow. I experience a tinge of dread.

The reason for my foreboding is something I have often discussed with one of my coworkers and fellow field representative, Fred. We have discussed that a male field rep faces a certain amount of risk when meeting alone with a female client in her home. For obvious reasons, Fred and I prefer it when there is another person present, be it a husband, relative, or a friend.

I have decided that if I run into a situation which I think is heading toward the possibility of the claimant acting improperly or placing me in an uncomfortable situation from a sexual standpoint, I'll simply get up, announce that the field visit is over, and depart. I've always feared that this nightmare scenario could become a dreaded reality for me if I don't exercise great care during solo interviews with female claimants.

I have not been privy to management instruction in this area, but I remain steadfast in my plan to flee any possible problem before it comes to fruition by driving a block or so away and calling the local police department. I'll then file a report to protect myself from any false accusations that might arise. Thankfully, nothing like this has happened to me in my nine-year field representative career. I didn't know it yet, but the next couple of days will change all of that.

CHAPTER 4

TUESDAY: THIRTEEN DAYS EARLIER

I'm up bright and early so I can leave the house by 7:00 a.m. to head for the car rental facility at the Atlanta airport. I have to give myself extra time for the infamous Atlanta traffic jams. With my sports coat, PC, claim file copy, and other essentials in tow, I depart for Helena in a rental car about 9:00 a.m. (EST). My trip is uneventful until I receive a call on my cell phone shortly after 11:00 a.m.

"This is Kevin Harrington. Can I help you?"

I then hear, "Hello, Mr. Harrington. This is Gayle Wade, and I hate to bother you."

"No bother, Ms. Wade. I'm planning on ringing your doorbell in about an hour."

She answers, "That's what I'd like to talk to you about. I know this is not much notice, but can we meet tomorrow instead of today?" I cringe since I'm in a rental car and am not that far from her house.

I think quickly and recall that my next client appointment is set for Thursday, the day after tomorrow. Therefore, in the interest of providing the best customer service possible, I say, "Sure, Ms. Wade, I can do that for you. Is the same time okay?"

After a slight hesitation, I hear, "Yes, noon will be good. I appreciate your being flexible. I've not left the house since my accident, but if we meet tomorrow, my boyfriend can be here."

I think to myself that this is a silver lining in this situation since it means I won't be alone with her during our conversation. "Very good then, Ms. Wade," "I'll see you tomorrow." She thanks me again and hangs up. I pull over to the side of the road to think about what I should do next.

I'm already in Alabama with a rental car and hate the idea of driving back for nothing. I have a lot of leeway with my schedule, so I decide to get a hotel room and work remotely for the rest of the day. I have several things I can do, and I'd prefer to avoid five hours of unproductive windshield time. Therefore, I stop at a Walmart and buy some new underwear, socks, and toiletries. I then sign on to the corporate website via my wireless connection and book a room at the Hoover, Alabama, Marriott. After checking in, I start on some tasks I can perform online.

By about 12:30 p.m., I go through the Wade file again. I decide to run a database check on her, something I had neglected to do earlier. This is done through the data warehouse website made available via the membership of my employer. I run a query, and wow, what a bonanza! I'm thankful she delayed the interview because I have several interesting hits on her background check.

The first thing of note is that Ms. Wade has used different names in the past. I've never run into this before. She has apparently gone by the names of Betty Gayle Bolton and Gayle Betty Ford in the past. She filed for bankruptcy in a Birmingham courtroom about three years ago. She also had a small civil judgment filed against her in the same year by a hospital. So it seems apparent she has had recent financial troubles.

She was also documented as having several addresses in the last few years, mostly in and around the Helena area. Then something even more interesting pops up. She's served time in an Alabama Department of Corrections (ADC) facility for an undisclosed amount of time before being released in early 2010. I was able to secure her ADC ID number, 386901.

Seeing indications of aliases and incarceration for Ms. Wade, I get a little pumped up and phone the claim examiner in Clearwater. I inform her of my findings, and she expresses her surprise at what I've turned up. I tell her I have the afternoon free and plan to do some exploring concerning a few other issues I saw in the claim documentation Ms. Wade filed. She wishes me luck and hangs up.

Thank God I have this free time today. I plan to check out some of her allegations in person, but I start by calling the ADC. It never ceases to amaze me that a caller can often get a ton of information over the phone simply by acting like he or she has a right to what is being requested. In fact, nearly nothing should ever be released over the phone or in person in the absence of the appropriate release form being in the hands of the person or agency holding personal information.

At any rate, I wind my way through the electronic phone answering system and am finally connected to the public information manager, Mr. Tim Zapf. I identify myself and inform Mr. Zapf that I am seeking information on Ms. Wade concerning her apparent incarceration in Alabama. Mr. Zapf confirms that Ms. Wade was held in the corrections system and was released from a state prison in 2010. This matches what I found in my search!

I asked Mr. Zapf if I could send him an authorization form signed by Ms. Wade as part of her claim submission, and he replies that he really doesn't need it. He says he would accept e-mail communication from me regarding any questions I have about Ms. Wade and answer them to the extent that his legal advisors give him approval for. I thank him for his cooperation and end the call after writing down his e-mail address. I immediately compose and mail an e-mail request to him asking for details of Ms. Wade's criminal background, her periods of incarceration, and the reasons she was arrested. I feel pretty good about my work so far in this matter.

It's only about 1:30 p.m., so I make a list of places I plan to go to in order to document the details of her disability claim. These include the Birmingham Police Department; the Circle K, where she fell; the hospital she said treated her after the accident; and her employer, M.B. Construction. This is an aggressive plan, so I depart the hotel.

I use my GPS to find the main office of the Birmingham Police Department. It's called Central Headquarters and is located in an older section of downtown. As I walk into the aged multi-story cement building, I see a lot of young men and women who I decide are probably keeping scheduled appointments with their parole officers or attending other legal-based required visits. No one bothers me in my preppy-looking sports coat and slacks as I make my way to the records department on the main floor.

There is no line, and the clerk introduces herself as Brenda. She takes the identifying information I provide concerning Ms. Wade and goes to a desk with a PC on it. She clicks away for a few minutes and then approaches the window where I'm waiting. She gives me a nine-digit case number, telling me it concerns a one-car wreck in 2011 involving Ms. Wade. She shared that Ms. Wade was driving eighty in a forty-five mile per hour zone and drove into an embankment.

Brenda tells me to wait a minute and goes into backroom behind her desk. She returns and hands me a copy of an accident report concerning the incident. I glance at it and affirm that Ms. Wade was the driver and sole occupant of the car. I see no indication of alcohol or drug use being involved in the incident. I thank Brenda and ask if there is any other information concerning Ms. Wade over the past few years available in the police records system.

Glancing around to be sure no one can hear, she replies, "Mr. Harrington, there are several other incidents and reports in our system for Ms. Wade, but they've been sealed by the courts." I asked what it would take to secure copies of them, and she whispers, "I can't release them without a subpoena. I wish I could help you, but I've already told you more than I'm supposed to." I thank Brenda for her help, take my copy of the

2011 Alabama traffic accident report she gave me, and leave the premises.

It's still only midafternoon, and I decide to run by the Circle K store where Ms. Wade reported she fell. I previously found the address in the claim information she submitted and used it to find the store's location on my GPS. I walk in with my digital camera in case there is a need to take pictures to help clarify the incident. I walk up to the clerk at the front and ask for the manager or owner. He replies that the owner, Mr. Gibson, is out but should return in a few minutes. I thank him and indicate I'll return in about thirty minutes.

To kill time more than anything else, I decide to go to the hospital that Ms. Wade reported she drove herself to immediately after her fall. Capstone Memorial Hospital is only about ten minutes from the Circle K. I'm armed with a copy of a medical release signed by Ms. Wade that the front desk clerk at the Marriott photocopied for me. I go directly to the medical records division, knowing that my chances of receiving records in person are slim to none.

I briefly explain to the hospital associate that I want to secure copies of the records of any treatment provided to Ms Wade on the day of her claimed accident, March 21, 2013. The employee, whose name badge identifies her as Joann Avicious, asks me to wait a minute and leaves the window. She returns about five minutes later and asks me if I'm sure Ms. Wade was a patient in March of 2013. Ms. Avicious tells me she searched the hospital database for all of 2012 and 2013, and there is no record of treatment for a Gayle Wade, or any females with the last name of Wade for that matter.

That's interesting, I think to myself. Ms. Avicious suggests that I complete a medical records request form right now and leave it and a copy of Ms. Wade's authorization with her. In this way, she explained, DPG will receive official confirmation from the hospital that there was no treatment rendered to Ms. Wade in 2013. I do as she suggests, thank her for her time, and return to the Circle K.

I go back to the Circle K, and the manager, Mr. Gibson, has returned. I explain that my employer is investigating a disability claim from a client who said she fell in his store on March 21. He raises his eyebrows and says, "Really? I never heard of anyone falling." He indicated that his store, a franchise operation, carries liability insurance for such occurrences, and no incidents have been reported or claimed so far this year.

Mr. Gibson further states there are cameras positioned throughout the store, and there is nowhere on-site that a fall could happen and go unrecorded. He did admit that someone could fall, not report it, and leave under their own power, in which case he and his employees would be none the wiser.

He confirms that surveillance tapes are kept for one year to meet requirements set by their liability insurance carrier. Per my request, Mr. Gibson agrees to review the tapes for the month of March 2013 and determine if anyone fell. I shared with him that Ms. Wade's claim submission indicated she fell near the front door. He agrees to review the tapes and call me on my cell phone if anything turns up. He indicates he can't promise anything, but he'll try to get this project done today. I thank him and head for my car.

I buckle in and glance at my watch. It's about 3:30 p.m., and instead of heading back to the hotel, I decide to try another long shot. Ms. Wade indicated in her claims information that her employer, MB Construction, is located at 1523 Crown Street in Birmingham. I decide to see what I can find out, if anything, from MB. I plug the address information into my GPS and draw a blank. That's certainly weird, but maybe I got something wrong.

I plug in just Crown Street with no number, and nothing matches, although there is a Crow Street. I try to enter 1523 Crow Street, and the closest location listed is 999 Crow Street. I drive to this location and find an old residential neighborhood that dead-ends at a house with the numbers 999 on the front. I'm headed back to the hotel when I see a large and active truck stop a few blocks away from Crow Street.

I pull in and walk up to the front cash register. There are cars gassing up at outside pumps, and several trucks are parked next to the building. A number of truck drivers are lounging in a restaurant near a large restroom. I ask the young pimply-faced cashier if she has heard of MB Construction, and she defers to an older man whom she calls over. Introducing him as her boss, she says he's worked here for thirty years and knows everything about this town.

I shake a proffered hand, and the elderly gentleman introduces himself as Sam Bradley. "What can I do for you?" he asks. I explain that I'm looking for MB Construction, and it's supposedly located at 1523 Crown Street. He smiles and replies, "I've lived in Birmingham all my life and never heard of a Crown Street. I'm pretty sure there is no such street."

"I also know pretty much every business in town, including ones that came and went years ago. I don't know of any MB Construction. Do you know if it's supposed to be on the south side of Birmingham or if it changed its name?" I respond that I know nothing more than I've told him. He looks me directly in the eye and adds, "I feel confident in telling you that there is no MB Construction in Birmingham and never has been. Have you tried to Google it?" I tell him I tried this and was unsuccessful. He shakes his head and notes, "That should tell you something in itself." I thank Mr. Bradley for his cooperation and leave the truck stop.

It was getting to be late afternoon, and I head back to my room at the Marriott. When I arrive, I check my company e-mail and answer a few inquiries. I eat dinner at about 7:00 p.m. and watch some mindless TV programming for a few hours. I go to bed at about 11:00 p.m. after hanging my shirt and slacks in the bathroom with the shower running only hot water and the door closed. I fall asleep thinking this case is becoming more and more interesting.

CHAPTER 5

WEDNESDAY: TWELVE DAYS EARLIER

I wake up at 7:30 a.m. and take a shower. Since I have minimal toiletries and no workout clothes, I defer to a session on the treadmill in the exercise room. I read the paper at breakfast in the grill next to the front lobby and decide to drop in again at the Circle K before proceeding to the meeting with Ms. Wade.

I stroll into the convenience store at about 10:00 a.m., and the manager, Mr. Gibson, is behind the counter. I approach him, and he announces, "Hey, I was going to call you. I watched all the tapes for the entire month of March. There was nothing recorded that documented any type of fall by a female customer. There are two cameras that cover the front door area, and I watched those tapes twice. I feel confident in saying there was no accidental fall inside the store. It's possible she could've fallen outside the front door, but we wouldn't catch that on tape." I thank Mr. Gibson and walk to my car, thinking that nothing about this claim is kosher at this point in time.

I head down Interstate 65 toward Helena. It will only take about forty-five minutes, but I want to take a look at her home and property before I go inside to talk with her. While driving, my mind drifts to my twelve-year career with DPG. The first few years, I comanaged a large disability claims operation with about three hundred employees. The work was grueling in nature and entailed long hours. But then the powers that be decided this location should be closed to take advantage of "centralized efficiencies."

I was devastated since I was at an age when it's difficult to find a good job. I was amazed at the number of people who worked for me who were thrilled that the company decided to offer settlement packages to everyone depending on one's job classification and tenure. I thought they were missing the boat because I considered a good job in hand preferable to a one-time payment.

At any rate, I was fortunate to parley my participation in an interoffice project with the individual disability claim office in Houston into a job offer to be a field representative. It was, and remains to be, a job made in heaven for me. For the first time in my working career, I have no management responsibility and only have to worry about my own performance.

The last nine years have been great and really interesting. The Wade claim seems to be, to this point, a good example of an interesting situation, offering the possibilities of discovering some collateral facts pertinent to the claim if I'm willing to take the time and effort to look for them.

I think back to some of my more interesting field visits in the past. My former boss, Randy Bryant, accompanied me on my initial training field visit. We made an appointment with a claimant in Jacksonville, Florida, who had been receiving benefit payments for a few years. This gentleman and his wife invited us to enter their condominium, which overlooked the bay near downtown. When he shut the front door, he yelled out with an Italian accent, "Do you want to see why I'm disabled? Do you want to know why?" I was speechless, as was Randy, and I didn't reply.

The claimant then removed his shirt and dropped his matching shorts and underwear. Naked as a jaybird, he pirouetted in a circle and shouted, "This is why I can't work. Take a look!" All over his body, with the exception of his face and head, were dark red splotches and skin rashes, some of which were bleeding slightly. His wife buried her eyes in her hands and shook her head.

As Randy remained silent, I stated to the claimant, "Okay, thank you, sir. I'm going to wait at your kitchen table until you get dressed and are ready to talk." Randy, the claimant's wife, and I went into the kitchen, and Randy gave me a slight wink and smile. The remainder of the interview and visit was uneventful, thank goodness.

A week after that, Randy called me and said, "Hey, Kevin. I just wanted to let you know that I talked to the claim office today and told them about your first field visit. I said that we entered this guy's condo after he met us at the door. I explained that his eyes met your eyes, and he stripped down to nothing." We shared a laugh over this, and I told him I wasn't looking forward to explaining this experience to the other field reps.

I briefly recalled two other visits of interest. The first of which was in Tennessee. I went to interview a gentleman with a mental disorder. Upon entering his small ranch-style residence, I found out he had twenty-six cats and was raising eight ferrets in the home. The ferrets were in cages in his living room, and the powerful stench made it difficult to breathe. I spoke with him while several of his cats walked on my shoulders and upper back.

This gentleman suggested we go into his kitchen to complete our discussion because it might be a little more comfortable. This room had the appearance of a committed hoarder, as there were boxes, books, and other items stacked on every flat surface. The walkway on the kitchen floor, tiled in red and white squares, was worn down to the underlying plywood. Also, I noted that his oven door was open, and it was filled to overflowing with books, papers, and other items, as if it were a bookcase. I was glad to leave his house and resume breathing fresh air again.

The other field visit I thought about briefly was an interview with an elderly retired school teacher in Mississippi. She was sweet and cooperative and rented a basement apartment as her retirement abode. She had two small white dogs named Foofie and Fifi. I was deep in conversation with her, taking detailed notes, when one of her dogs put its icy-cold tongue about halfway between my ankle and knee inside my pant leg. Startled, I yelled out and toppled over backward in a wingback chair. She chastised Foofie but couldn't contain a grin that morphed into laughter at my reaction to being "kissed" by her dog.

At any rate, my mind returned to the present as my GPS informs me I am only a half mile away from the home of Ms. Wade. I anticipate a potentially interesting visit based on my preliminary investigation. I have no idea how interesting things will become.

NOON: THE WADE FIELD VISIT

I pull up to her house, a one-story frame structure on a dead-end road in a thickly wooded area. Her home appears to be no bigger than six hundred square feet and is accessible via a gravel driveway. There is no garage. The yard needs to be mowed but is otherwise unremarkable.

An old unplated Camaro is parked in the driveway and looks as if it has not been in service for some time. I ring the doorbell, and a thirty-something white man invites me inside. He introduces himself as Bob Ireland and indicates he is Ms. Wade's boyfriend. He then says, "Gayle's bedfast, and you'll need to go to the bedroom to talk to her."

A red flag goes off in my head, and I ask Mr. Ireland, "You'll be in the room with us, won't you?"

He smiles and responds, "Sure."

I notice a small living room, a smaller kitchen, and a bathroom as we go to the back of the home to the bedroom. It appears to be a one-bedroom, one-bath residence. The interior of the house is dirty and in a state of disarray. Clothes and boxes are strewn in the hallway and all over the place.

Ms. Wade is sitting up in bed, with a sheet covering her from her feet to her waist. She is wearing a pajama top that shows a lot of cleavage. She is a white woman who appears to be about 5'4" and 190 pounds. She has thick shoulder-length hair and a full face. She appears to be her stated age of thirty-eight years old.

After presenting her with my business card, I move toward the only chair in the small room, which is situated near the headrest of the bed. With Ms. Wade's permission, I move it to the foot of the bed. During our discussion, she alternates from sitting up to lying down in a prone position. A few times, she removes the sheet, and I note she is wearing matching pajama bottoms and white socks. Although she frequently changes positions, she never stands up.

A large-screen TV is on a chest of drawers in the corner of the room. There are piles of clothes, as well as empty water bottles, Coke bottles, and candy wrappers, on the floor. Her self-proclaimed boyfriend, Mr. Ireland, remains standing in the doorway during the field visit but observes only and doesn't participate in the interview. Ms. Wade appears to be comfortable during our discussion, although she claims her back bothers her now and then.

As is my usual routine, I ask for permission to photograph her driver's license and health insurance ID card. She says she doesn't have any health insurance but reaches into her purse, which is sitting on the bed. She hands me what appears to be a driver's license. However, upon closer inspection, it is actually an Alabama non-driver identification card.

Recalling that the police department gave me a copy of a 2011 accident report in which she was driving, I ask her why she doesn't have a driver's license. She says, "I haven't had a license in a long time." I asked why, and she replied, "I just haven't needed one. Bob takes me where I need to go. It's a common thing for people to have state ID cards that are for identification only and not driver's licenses." I inform her that she is the first person I have interviewed in nine years with a non-driver's ID card. She does not reply to this statement.

I ask her to explain what happened at the Circle K in March.

She starts drawing patterns on her bed covers, not meeting my gaze. "I went into the store to buy a pack of cigarettes. I was by myself. I slipped on the floor somehow. It may have been wet. I don't really know. I fell backward on my back. An employee asked if he could help me and offered to call paramedics or an ambulance. I said no and called Bob instead."

"How did you get to the store?" I interject.

Her fingers freeze mid-pattern. When she spoke, her voice wavered a bit, "A-a-a friend dropped me off, and I planned to call Bob to pick me up."

Her story sounded a bit off, but I gestured for her to go on.

"Bob showed up in about ten minutes and took me to the emergency room."

"At Capstone?"

"Yes." She then relates, "Before Bob showed up, the store employee brought me a chair to sit in."

"Ms. Wade, did you go to the Capstone emergency room on the same day as you fell?"

She nods but then says, "No, wait a minute. Bob took me home and then we went to the ER a day or so later."

I ask her if this means she was at Capstone on March 22 or March 23, and she responds vaguely, "Yes, on one of those days."

I request that she tell me the names of the emergency physician or personnel who treated her, and she says, "I can't remember." I ask why she waited one or two days to go to the hospital, and she explains it was because she was still in pain.

"Ms Wade, were you kept overnight at Capstone?"

She answers, "No, I stayed for one or two hours, and they gave me a pain shot." I ask what type of medicine they gave her, and she responds that it was some type of anti-inflammatory, but she wasn't sure.

Moving our talk along, I ask Ms. Wade to identify the physician who is treating her back injury. She replies that she is treated by Dr. Clay Stevenson, an orthopedic surgeon in Birmingham. She continues that Dr. Stevenson told her she had a back sprain and gave her an injection of something. She indicates she had a second injection just last week. I inquire if she has engaged in any type of work activity since she fell on March 21, and she replies, "No, I haven't worked since then. In fact, I've been bedfast since that time."

I confirm the name and address of Dr. Stevenson with Ms. Wade and also the name of her primary care physician and her gynecologist. I ask if she has any other health issues affecting her ability to work, and she replies, "No." I then request that she tell me about any back discomfort and her restrictions. She says, "My back pain is constant and feels like a burning sensation. I get some relief from taking medications, having Bob massage my back, and using a heating pad."

I ask if she can walk or stand, and she responds, "Walking or standing for more than a few minutes makes my back burn." She also confirms that she spends twenty-two or twenty-three hours a day in bed. I ask her if this pattern has been unchanged since the fall, and she confirms this to be the case. I asked if Dr. Stevenson recommended any physical therapy, and she said, "Yes, he did. I went to one session in his office but haven't been back." I asked why, and she stated, "I can't afford it."

For the benefit of the claim department, I confirm all of Ms. Wade's medications and the address of the pharmacy she uses. I note she claims to be taking Gabapentin and Percocet for her pain. She also reports that she only walks short distances in her house because she is afraid of falling. She added that she is not able to perform any household chores, and stooping and bending make her back sore.

I reopen an earlier subject and ask Ms. Wade if she is able to drive a car. She frowns and says, "I don't drive." I press her on this and again ask why she doesn't have a driver's license. She remains tight-lipped in this area and pointedly says, "There is no reason. I just don't drive."

I then ask, "Have you had some type of legal trouble that caused your driver's license to be revoked?"

She is adamant in her response, explaining, "There's no particular reason I don't drive, I just don't. It's not that unusual, you know."

I drop this subject and move on. She affirms, again, that Bob takes her everywhere she needs to go, including medical appointments. She adds that her 2–3 doctor visits a month represent the only times she has left her home since the accident. We then cover her social activities, which she claims are limited to visiting her adult children from a previous marriage on rare occasions.

I now bring up the subject of her reported employer, MB Construction. She confirms that she has worked there for eight years as an accountant and, for the last two years, as their CFO. I share with her that I was unable to locate MB Construction and ask her to tell me the exact street address for the company. This request seems to make her nervous, and she says, "I'm not good at remembering the names of streets. I just go to work via memory."

I ask how she got to work before the fall, and she explains that a coworker picked her up and took her home. I tell her that I can't find a Crown Street in Birmingham, and she looks confused but remains silent. I ask her to give me directions from her home to MB Construction, and she replies, "Take Highway 80, or is it 81, to the Millwood Exit. Yes, make that Highway 80 to Millwood. Turn right at the exit and drive till you see a Shell station. Continue around that curve to the left, and bear right. You'll see a lot of trucking companies. Go three more blocks, and you're there."

Assessing that these directions are a little vague, I ask if she can find the address of her employer on any paperwork in her house or on her PC. "No, I can't," she responds a little quickly. I ask if she can remember the names of any of the trucking companies near MB so I can try to plug one of them into my GPS, and she replies, "No, I can't remember any of them."

I state to her, "Ms. Wade, you said you worked there for eight years, right?"

She looks me in the eyes and says, "That's right."

Deciding not to beat a dead horse, I ask her to tell me about the company, including the number of employees and her specific duties. "There are eight employees, including myself and the owner, Mr. Brown. There's also an administrative assistant and an office manager. The others are laborers," she replies in a shaky voice. I ask what her salary is, and she states it is about $8,000 per month, but she hasn't been paid since she fell.

I ask her what the monthly payroll for MB Construction is, and she estimates it to be $20,000. This seems unlikely to me if she usually receives $8,000 for her salary alone. She also reports the company's gross annual revenues for the last two years have been in the area of $300,000. I ask her to identify one of MB's main customers, and she says the City of Birmingham is a big one.

Ms. Wade went on to tell me she worked 8:00 a.m. till 5:00 p.m. on Mondays through Fridays. She explained that since it's a small company, she issues invoices to the customers. I ask how many she issues a month, and she says, "Ten to twelve, and they have thirty days to pay us." She continues that she also answers the phone and tracks the hours worked by the other employees.

I ask what percentage of MB's work is performed for the city of Birmingham, and she estimates it is about 20 percent and consists mostly of land-clearing activities. She adds that the company also hauls gravel and builds additions for churches.

I wrap up discussion about her employment by asking her if she plans to return to work. A frown forms on her face and she responds, "Yes, when I get better. I don't know when that will be." I still have doubts that MB Construction exists. Although there seems to be holes in her story, I'm impressed with Ms. Wade's ability to talk the talk.

I ask her if she has any income sources at the present, and she indicates she does not. She also affirms that she has not filed for Social Security Disability, workers' compensation, or state unemployment benefits. Additionally, she says she hasn't applied for any community assistance programs. Ms. Wade then reports that she received a business degree from the University of Alabama in 2000. I asked if she has any professional licenses or designations, and she reports that she is a certified public accountant in Alabama. I wonder if this is true, but I don't question her further in this matter. She repeats that she wants to return to work as soon as possible, but she has to get rid of her back pain and recover her strength.

At this time, I make a request of Ms. Wade that DPG field reps are authorized to employ when there is doubt concerning some of the information presented by a claimant. I ask her if she will answer some questions for me in writing via a signed document. To my surprise, she agrees to do so. She asks if I can record her answers for her instead of her doing the writing herself because the act of writing tires her. I agree to this, and we begin.

I ask her if she has ever had a driver's license in any state suspended or revoked. She replies, "No." I ask if she has ever had any legal charges filed against her or if she has been convicted of a felony or misdemeanor, and she again says, "No." I then ask if she has ever served time in a prison or any type of penal institution in Alabama, and she firmly responds, "No." I take this line of questioning one more step and ask if she was released from any prison or correctional facility in 2010. She tells me she has never been incarcerated for any reason and, interestingly enough, doesn't ask me why I am pursuing this line of questioning.

I record all of her these answers on a DPG carbonless form, allowing me to leave a copy of her statement with her. I add the following sentence to the bottom of the statement: "I certify that, to the best of my knowledge, the above is true and accurate." Per my request, Ms. Wade reviews the statement and then signs and dates it. I am amazed that she is willing to do this because I'm pretty confident that she is affirming statements that are false.

I inform Ms. Wade that I have gathered all of the information I need to write a field report for the claim department to assist them in adjudicating her disability claim. I ask her if there is anything she wishes to add to what she has told me or if she wants to make any changes to her answers, and she smiles and says, "No, Mr. Harrington." She then sits up and reaches out to shake my hand as I prepare to leave. She assumes a sitting position while doing this, and when I lean slightly downward to shake her hand, she suddenly grabs the back of my neck and plants a kiss on my cheek.

This is totally inappropriate, and I quickly jerk backward and stand up straight. I look behind me, and Mr. Ireland is still standing in the doorway, and he is grinning. I say to both of them, "What the heck is going on here?"

Ms. Wade replies, "Nothing. I guess us Southerners are prone to kiss people on the cheek when we say good-bye. I didn't mean anything by it."

Somehow, the tone of her voice doesn't ring true, but I was uncomfortable and ready to leave. I blustered, "Okay, thanks for talking to me," and quickly leave the bedroom and the house.

I get into my rental car and drive a mile or so before pulling over to the side of the road. I think to myself that maybe I should call the police and initiate an incident report. However, my male ego gets in the way as I cringe at the thought of telling a cop that I was uncomfortable when a woman kissed me. He'd probably think I was wimpy or something, especially when he learns that the lady's boyfriend was in the room at the time. Going against the little voice in my head, I decide to let it go and drive off toward Birmingham.

2:30 P.M.

I feel that I have the makings of one heck of a field report that might become a real feather in my cap to management. I'm ready to drive back to Atlanta and drop off the rental car but recall that Ms. Wade had given me some vague directions for finding MB Construction. I pull over again and refer to my notes. I find the section in which she stated she travelled to work by going from her house to Highway 80 and looking for the Millwood Exit.

I stop at a gas station and am directed to Highway 80. When I find it, I'm not sure which direction to go. I plug in the intersection of Highway 80 and Millwood into my GPS and get a hit. I head north on 80, which is in the general direction of Birmingham. I find the exit and turn right as Ms. Wade had instructed. I see a Shell station within a mile and continue onward. I come upon a sweeping curve to the left that goes upward to a hill. However, I see no chance to bear right as she had indicated. I find one trucking company, not a lot of them, as Ms. Wade had promised.

I drive on and come to the end of Millwood at a T intersection. I return to the trucking company I had found— AA Trucking—and go into the lobby. The receptionist says she hasn't heard of MB Construction Company in the area or in Birmingham proper. I thank her and head back out to the car. I pick up my small handheld recorder and document my attempt to find MB for reference purposes when I begin working on my report in a few days. Little did I realize that I wouldn't be writing up this visit at all, much less in the near future.

CHAPTER 6

WEDNESDAY: 3:30 P.M.

I decide to start back to the Atlanta area since I'm scheduled to fly to Raleigh in the morning. I also intend to make some phone call attempts on the way. I do this as much as possible to use my windshield time more effectively. Often, I'm able to garner information in this manner which I document via my little recorder. I feel this is a good use of my time as it often relieves me of making calls from my home office, freeing me up for dictation, appointment scheduling, etc.

The first contact I make is with the City of Birmingham. I call 411 and am connected to a general contact number for the city. I tell the person answering I want to speak with someone who might be able to confirm some work performed for the city by an outside construction company. I'm connected to a Sally in the licensing and vendor division. I ask if I can confirm that MB Construction is authorized to perform jobs for the city and if they have done so in the past few years. To my mild surprise, Sally asks me to wait a few minutes while she checks city records. I am continually amazed how much information I am able to retrieve over the phone.

She returns a few minutes later and tells me she can find no record of an MB Construction being an approved city vendor or performing any work for the city. She adds that they previously used an MT Construction several years ago, and this company was based in Montgomery, Alabama. I ask if MB Construction was ever licensed to do work for the city and what kind of jobs they performed in the past. Sally informs me that she can't divulge any more information about city records over the phone. I thank her for her assistance and end the call. I think to myself that this is one more kink in the armor of Ms. Wade's story as I document my findings on my recorder.

Next, I decide to try to confirm Ms. Wade's reported educational background. Utilizing AT&T information again, I am connected to the registrar's office at the University of Alabama in Tuscaloosa, Alabama. I briefly explain to a clerk that I'm trying to confirm that an individual graduated from the university with a business degree in or around 2000. I give her Ms. Wade's name, and she asks me to hold for a little while.

The clerk returns to the phone and informs me that no one named Gayle Wade attended or graduated from the University of Alabama from 1980 through the present. I am beginning to expect no collaboration for anything I check out. I press my luck and ask the clerk if she can check out the aliases I believe Ms. Wade has used in the past.

She agrees to look for any records of Betty Gayle Bolton and Gayle Betty Ford, the aliases that turned up in connection with Ms. Wade in the database check I ran yesterday. The agreeable clerk puts me on hold again for a few minutes before returning and informing me that no students under these names have attended the university either. I thank her for her cooperation, end the call, and duly record my findings on my recorder.

I'm still an hour from Atlanta on Interstate 20 East and decide to make one more call and see if my luck holds on information gathering. I ask the information operator if she can find a state CPA organization for Alabama. She said she doesn't usually do this for customers, but she'll look. I tell her how much I appreciate her efforts, and she places me on hold. I'm nearly ready to hang up, thinking the operator has forgotten me, when she comes back on line and tells me there is an Alabama Society of CPAs. She asks me which office I wish to be connected to, and I ask if there is one in Tuscaloosa. She replies that there isn't but that there is one in Birmingham. I ask to be connected to this branch and thank her again for helping me.

Once again, I seemed to be leading a charmed life. I go through a receptionist and am connected to an administrative assistant, a Ms. Yarnell. I inform her that I am assisting a customer with a disability insurance claim matter, and it will be helpful to know if she is a registered CPA in Alabama. She tells me it will take her a few minutes to check this out, and I tell her I'm happy to wait on hold.

She returns to the line about five minutes later and tells me that Ms. Wade is not now nor has she ever been a CPA in the state of Alabama. I ask her if she will check under the names of Betty Gayle Bolton and Gayle Betty Ford. I hear her exhale with apparent frustration, and she says to hold for a few more minutes. She comes back soon and affirms that no one by these additional names is a CPA in Alabama either. I thank her, end the call, and record these findings. Man, what a report this is going to turn out to be!

CHAPTER 7

WEDNESDAY: 8:30 P.M.

After turning in my rental car at the airport and riding a train to the terminal and a bus to my off-site airport parking lot, I head for home. I arrive home at about 9:30 p.m. thinking about my early morning flight to Raleigh. After giving my dogs a few minutes of petting and soothing talk, I head upstairs to hook up my PC and check for any messages. I also intend to go to the Delta website and send a boarding pass for the morning flight to my cell phone.

I see a message on my work landline and simultaneously notice a message on my home landline. I glance at my cell phone and notice a message on it, and only then do I realize that I apparently turned off the ringtone sometime earlier in the day. I check my landline first and am shocked to hear a message from my boss in Houston. I can't imagine what happened that he would call my home number. He says to call him today no matter how late I get this message.

I check the work landline message and hear almost the same message verbatim. Now I'm getting nervous. I check my cell and, and as I now expect, the message is also from my boss. I think for a second and remember the uncomfortable moment when Ms. Wade landed a wet one on my cheek. Now I wish to high heaven I'd called the police when I left her home and filed an incident report. Oh well, the best laid plans and all that.

I open a can of Coke and take a swig. Then, I pick up my work landline and call my boss. He answers on the third ring. "This is Doug Wills."

I feel uneasy as I detect some apprehension in his usually calm voice and demeanor. "Doug, this is Kevin. You asked that I call. Is everything all right?"

"Kevin, did you have some trouble at a field visit today? I believe you visited a Gayle Wade?"

"Yes, a little, Doug, and I should have taken some action to include calling you about it, but I didn't."

Raising his voice slightly, Doug says, "Tell me what happened and then I'll tell you what's happened on this end." My heart begins racing, and my stomach starts to churn. I try to gather myself and then give him a recap of what took place from the minute I entered the Wade house until I left. I include my consideration of contacting the police and regretting that I didn't, especially since something must have happened after I left.

Doug then tells me, "Ms. Wade called our corporate office in Houston and asked for the president. She eventually was connected to the legal department. You may remember Buster

Todd. He handles most of our legal issues for us. Buster told her he was the primary attorney for the claim department. She proceeded to tell him that you tried to assault her in some manner during the interview." He hesitated briefly, and I was temporarily speechless. I felt a combination of anger, fear, and helplessness.

"Are you still there?" asks Doug.

I tried to sound calm as I reply, "I'm here, and that is pure BS."

I must have sounded upset because Doug retorts, "Take it easy, Kevin. We'll get to the bottom of this."

I then blurt out, "Her damn boyfriend was there the whole time and knows I didn't do anything wrong. Is he lying too?"

I hear Doug exhale and say, "I don't know all of what she said, but I believe she told Buster that he stepped out of the room for a minute and was surprised to find her crying when he returned."

Now, my head is spinning, and I ask, "When can I tell my side of this? Man, I'm supposed to fly to Raleigh early in the morning."

I notice a nervous edge in Doug's voice as he asserts, "Kevin, I don't want you going in the field tomorrow. And I need to tell you that you can't conduct any more field visits until this thing is cleared up."

At that point, you could've knocked me over with a feather. I reply, "Doug, I didn't do anything wrong except use some poor judgment when I didn't call you and the cops. She's a damn liar!"

He tries to settle me down and calmly implores, "Kevin, take it easy. Legal made it clear you can't continue to work until this is straightened out. I'm going to have one of the claim examiners call the two claimants in the Raleigh area and reschedule them with other field reps." This hurt a lot! My colleagues are going to cover for me like I'm sick or something.

Doug continues, "I'm not telling anyone in the office why you're being placed on leave, and I suggest you keep this to yourself."

"Okay, am I still going to get paid?"

He exhales again and replies, "It's my understanding you are. But you need talk to Buster in the morning. He wants to hear your side of things and can answer any other questions you have."

Although it feels, and probably sounds, hollow, I say, "Doug, I'm really sorry about this. You know I love my job and my company. I'll do whatever it takes to make this right and get back in the saddle."

Instead of affirming me, Doug only offers, "We'll get to the bottom of this problem and make sure the company's liability and its reputation is protected."

I'm thinking, *What about me and my reputation?* but I just croak, "Thanks, Doug. Do I need to call you after I speak with Buster?"

He answers, "No, I'll be kept in the loop if the powers that be approve it." This seems like another vote of no confidence, but I thank him and hang up. My God, how will I sleep tonight?

CHAPTER 8

THURSDAY: ELEVEN DAYS EARLIER

9:00 A.M.

I finally get up after a night of tossing and turning. I'm a bit of a nervous Nellie by nature, and I splash cold water in my face after getting almost no sleep. My alarm went off at 4:30 a.m. because shortly after getting home, I had set it in anticipation of getting up to shower, pack, and go to the airport. Another sign I'm not myself is I put on a pair of good slacks and a nice golf shirt. I walk into the kitchen and realize I'm overdressed for a day at home; I feel like I'm falling apart.

I have a small panic attack and worry that I've forgot to call the Disability Protection Group attorney at a prearranged time. To the best of my recollection, I was only instructed to call in the morning. I grab my work cell phone and dial the Houston office. I ask for the legal department and identify myself to the receptionist. She asks me to wait a minute. I notice my hands are shaking, and it seems like a long time before Mr. Todd comes onto the line. I keep reminding myself that I haven't done anything wrong.

"Hello. Is this Kevin Harrington?" he asks.

My mouth feels parched and dry as I reply, "Yes, this is he."

He clears his throat and continues, "It appears that we have a little problem on our hands. A Birmingham attorney contacted us yesterday and informed us that he intends to file a complaint with the local police against you and the company alleging sexual abuse in the first degree during your visit with his client, Ms. Wade. The vice president of your claim office has told me you've been an exemplary employee, and there has never been any complaints filed against you during your tenure with DPG covering, I believe, nine years as a field representative.

"This situation is being looked at very seriously by the company. As you probably know, we have strict written employee guidelines concerning sexual harassment, misconduct, and inappropriate behavior on company grounds and when representing DPG in the public." I remain quiet even though I want to protest my innocence right now. He then asks the sixty-four million dollar question. "Is there any merit to the claim being made by Ms. Wade's attorney?"

I take a deep breath and say, "Absolutely not. I did nothing wrong. She remained in her bed during our conversation—"

Before I could finish, he blurts out, "You interviewed this woman in her bedroom? Tell me you didn't!"

I hear my voice crack slightly as I say, "Yes, per her request. She said she's been bedfast since a fall a few months ago. I think her claim is pure BS, but my job is to gather facts, not make claim decisions. Also, you should know that a guy she said is her boyfriend was present the whole time. And one more thing, when I stood up and walked over to shake her hand before leaving, she leaned forward, grabbed my neck, and kissed me on the cheek. It happened so fast, I couldn't avoid it."

There was uncomfortable silence on the other end of the phone before he states, "This doesn't sound too good. In the first place, I would never recommend or approve of an interview being conducted in a customer's bedroom. There are just too many risk factors in such a situation. But that's water under the bridge now. Did you, for any reason, expect her to kiss you or show any other type of affection?"

I adamantly respond, "Heck no. I was shocked that she did it, and I pulled away immediately. She had a big grin on her face. Almost like she was going to laugh at me. Looking back, I feel like she may have been setting me up."

"She may have been," Mr. Todd indicates.

I then confide, "Mr. Todd, I pulled over to the side of the road after I left her house and almost called 911 to report what happened. Now I feel I made a mistake by not doing this, and I also should have notified my boss. I just didn't envision anything coming of it. I thought she would say she routinely kisses people on the cheek when saying good-bye if I made an issue of it. I didn't want to look like an idiot when no harm seemed to have been done. Man, I wish I had listened to the little warning voice in my head."

Again, there is silence on the other end. I notice I'm sweating through my clothes. Mr. Todd finally speaks, "Look, I've arranged for local representation for you in case her lawyer follows through with his threat. I'm supposed to call him at 2:00 p.m. CST today. Is there anything you haven't told me about the interview?"

I reply quickly, "No, there's nothing else. But I want to tell you how sorry I am this happened. This is the best job I've ever had, and I'd hate to put my employment with Disability Protection Group in jeopardy."

If I was hoping for any soothing words, they didn't materialize. I then take about forty-five minutes going through my notes and telling Mr. Todd everything that happened over the last two days, including my contacts with other sources as well as the interview. I feel better when I finished, thinking that maybe laying everything on the table would make me seem legitimate somehow. It didn't seem to register with Mr. Todd as far as I can tell, and he instructs me, "I want you to FedEx everything you have to me—all of your notes and your recorder with your verbal statements connected to the Wade matter."

I write down his address after agreeing to send him everything I have. I don't bother asking him if I should go ahead and write up my report; I think I know the answer. He then makes sure I have his direct phone number, and he warns me, "Don't discuss this situation with anyone, not coworkers, friends, or family members. Especially don't talk to Ms. Wade's attorney if he calls you. If you get called by the police, give them my name and number so I can refer them to local counsel. And keep in mind, there's a chance this whole matter may be dropped. To my knowledge, I'm the only person that has been contacted so far." I say nothing in return as I don't see myself being this lucky.

I thank Mr. Todd for his help and confirm that I'll send my notes and handheld recording device to him via overnight delivery by midafternoon. I hang up the phone and feel a throbbing headache coming on. I walk into my living room and let my dogs outside in the backyard. I then sit on the coach and cry like a baby for a good ten minutes.

3:00 P.M.

I drive up to a Federal Express office with my notes and tape recorder. Before I left, I spent an hour or so photocopying my notes and typing the comments from my recorder on a Word document. I don't know why I did this, but I think I might need my own copy of them at some point so I play it safe. I have the FedEx clerk package the documents and address them to Mr. Todd. I hand him my company American Express card to pay for the postage. I wonder if my card will be cancelled soon.

I drive back home and wonder what I'm going to do with myself until this is cleared up. I have no idea how long this process can take, even if no charges are filed. When I get back home, I have a message on my home phone voice mail. I press the playback button with a shaky finger, and I hear this: "Mr. Harrington, this is Detective Skirvin of the Birmingham Police Sex Crimes Unit. I wanted to let you know that a local attorney, Matthew Geary, has filed a complaint against you for his client, Gayle Wade. I don't have any questions for you right now, but you are a person of interest to us. If you have an attorney or engage the services of one, I'd appreciate being informed as soon as possible. I can be reached through the main number of the Birmingham Police Department. Thank you. Bye." I play the message three times, and each time, I feel more nauseous.

I hang up and call Mr. Todd to inform him. He's in a meeting, and I tell the receptionist about the message. I let my dogs out again and hear the phone ring. Since it's my home phone, I'm not sure whether or not it's Buster. I run to the phone and hear the voice mail engage. I hear the message being left, and it is a solicitation call. I let the caller finish and then delete it without playing it back.

It's after 5:00 p.m. when Mr. Todd calls me back. "I got your message from my assistant," he begins. "Now we know Ms. Wade has chosen to proceed with legal action, which I figured she would do. I've engaged the services of a Birmingham attorney for you. His name is Ken Patterson, and he comes well recommended. He has a variety of experience in family law, criminal law, and other areas. Have you got a pen and paper to write down his address and phone number?" I put the phone down for a minute and grab something to write on. I record Mr. Patterson's information despite my trembling hand.

"Mr. Patterson would like you to call him tomorrow after 1:00 p.m.," he said. "I'd like to reiterate that I am recommending you not discuss this matter with anyone except me and Mr. Patterson. There is a possibility that the press could find out about this and publish the plaintiff's account of what happened." I think my heart stops beating when I hear this. He adds, "Please refer any contacts from any newspapers or other news media outlets to me no matter what questions or accusations are presented to you." I promised to do as he requested and end the call. Its dinnertime, but I'm not hungry.

Later, I'm sitting in front of my 42" HD TV, but I am not really watching it. I notice the Braves are beating the Marlins 4–3, when my home phone rings. It's my eighty-eight-year-old mother in Indiana. She is healthy as a horse and sharp for her age. She immediately picks up on my unsettled demeanor. "What's wrong, hon?" she asks. I tell her that everything is okay, and she then asks me what state I'm travelling to next for my job. I lie and tell her that I have some local appointments over the next couple of weeks that I can drive to without flying. We end the call a few minutes later, but I can tell she is worried that I'm holding something back from her. I justify being tight-lipped with my mom due to the instructions I received from Mr. Todd. It's kind of a gag order, I think to myself.

CHAPTER 9

FRIDAY: TEN DAYS EARLIER

8:30 A.M.

I get up after another restless night. I shower but skip shaving since I have no one to interview or nowhere to go. After taking my dogs outside, I decide to mow my grass and edge and trim my bushes—activities I usually perform on weekends. I hope that some physical activity will numb my mind a little. It doesn't work.

I come inside at about 11:45 a.m., take another shower, and put on a tee shirt, shorts, and tennis shoes. I start to make myself a sandwich when I notice my home landline voice mail light blinking. As I listen to the message, my gut starts to wrench. "Mr. Harrington, this is Jim Kendall of the *Birmingham Sentinel.* We have some information that you are being accused of a sexual assault deriving from an incident a couple of days ago. I thought you might want to give us your side of what happened before we print something about it. If I've reached the wrong person, please disregard this message." He then leaves me a number to call him back.

I take a second to put my head between my knees and breathe deeply. It doesn't seem to help, as my heart races, and I'm sweating through my shirt. I call Mr. Todd, and thankfully, reach him right away. He says, "I'm sorry that happened, but it doesn't surprise me. A reporter could have found out by reviewing courthouse filings, or Ms. Wade's attorney could have leaked the information to the paper to generate publicity. I'm going to contact the corporate information officer and advise her of what took place. She'll decide whether or not it's in our best interests for us to call this Kendall guy back. You just sit tight, you hear me?"

I reply that I do hear him, but I'm pretty worried. He again tells me it's important to let him and Mr. Patterson handle everything for me, including all communications. Feeling like a robot, I hear myself give my agreement to his instructions, and we end the call. I lie on my couch and wrap my arms around my head. How did all of this happen to me? What have I done to deserve this? I consider making an appointment with the pastor of my church but decide against it right now. Frankly, I don't want to tell him or anyone else what I've been accused of doing. I also note that it's no longer of help telling myself I didn't do anything wrong. It seems like that little fact doesn't matter.

Shortly after 1:00 p.m., I call Mr. Patterson. The conversation is short, and he seems a little cranky to me. I tell him about being contacted by the reporter, and he indicates he heard about this from Mr. Todd. I ask if he can do anything to help in this area, and he says there is nothing he can do and that "rag of a paper" will publish whatever it wants in order to sell more papers. What a comforting response.

I ask if he wants me to recount what happened when I visited Ms. Wade. He responds that Mr. Todd has filled him in, and he'll contact me if he needs more information. He then says he has an important meeting to attend, and he can't give me any more time. Feeling anything but warm and fuzzy, I hang up. I think to myself that this guy isn't interested in me, and I wish I had a different local lawyer. I plan to communicate this to Mr. Todd the next time we talk.

I spend the rest of the afternoon feeling sorry for myself. I take my dogs for a walk and later surf the Internet. I verify that the *Birmingham Sentinel* has a webpage and bookmark it. There is nothing of interest in it right now, but I note they have a Local Crime Page. Oh great. I order a pizza to be delivered and decide to watch a movie on TV in the evening. I feel like I'm sitting on a powder keg that may go off at any time. As it turns out, I'm right.

CHAPTER 10

SATURDAY: NINE DAYS EARLIER

After yet another restless night, I eat breakfast with my good friend and neighbor early on Saturday morning at a local greasy spoon. Noel and I have been close since I moved to my house twelve years ago. He, his wife, and teenage daughter have been supportive of me since my wife died. They invite me over to eat often. During breakfast, he asks me if something is bothering me since I'm so quiet. I tell him everything is fine, but I sense he doesn't believe me.

Later in the day, I catch a two-hour nap, which is really unusual for me. I know that my lack of sleep over the past three nights is the reason I fall asleep. I feel refreshed when I wake up until I remember my troubles again. I want to confront Ms. Wade badly, but I know this would be a huge mistake, be it in person or on the phone. I talk to my kids on Saturday night and do a pretty good job of seeming normal. I ask them questions and prompt them to talk about what's going with them, which allows me to be quiet and not talk much.

Late in the evening, I check CNN and Fox News on my cable TV system. There's nothing big out of Alabama, thankfully. I again check the *Sentinel* website, and it has nothing in it about Ms. Wade. I sign off and go to bed at about 11:00 p.m. I have to be up at 7:00 a.m. and get ready to attend church and teach a Sunday school class for tenth-grade boys. I review the lesson materials briefly before going to sleep. I wake up several times in a heavy sweat but manage to get some rest.

CHAPTER 11

SUNDAY: EIGHT DAYS EARLIER

I always enjoy Sundays. I go to church, see a lot of friends, eat lunch with some of them, and also teach a Sunday school class. In the afternoons, I find something fun to do like walking the dogs at a park or shopping for a lawn maintenance tool I don't really need. Last year, I purchased a gas-powered, commercial-grade hedge trimmer. The damn thing cost $390 and weighs almost sixty pounds. After using it for ten minutes, I have to rest it on my shoulder to hoist it high enough to sculpt my bushes. One slip, and I'm sure I'll lose an arm or a leg, but I love its ferocious roar and cutting power.

After my wife passed away a couple of years ago, I was afraid I wouldn't like Sundays since we did everything together on that day, even if she only wanted to rest at home. But, surprisingly, I still like the relaxed nature of the day and have learned to go solo pretty well, although I pretty much don't cook. Generally, I heat up frozen meals or go out to eat.

I drive to church at about 9:00 a.m. with a lot of worries clouding my thoughts. I ponder how my friends and cochurch members will react if the accusation against me goes viral. I try to push this thought out of my head as I park and enter the sanctuary. I haven't dated anyone since Linda passed away but have noticed I seem to be more attracted to the opposite sex in recent months. Unfortunately, the women I now find attractive tend to be 15–20 years younger than me and have children. I tell myself I need to face the fact I may never have a relationship with another woman, but this possibility doesn't really bother me.

After church, I talk to friends and head over to the Youth House to teach. I teach with another guy and try to keep the sessions entertaining and not a hundred percent serious. In this way, I hope that some of what we discuss sticks with these fifteen- and sixteen-year-old boys. I always start my lessons with a joke, and I'm certain that I'll be removed as a teacher if any of them ever reach the ears of the church staff.

As I enter the room, I notice there are eight boys present today. I ask them, one by one, to tell me and the rest of the class anything of interest that happened to them during the last week, in particular things like being questioned by the cops or being served with a paternity suit. They laugh, and most of them relate their experiences over the last week. One boy, who works in a fast-food chicken restaurant, always has a story to share about clashing with his coworkers or the customers. Today, he talks about a catfight he says took place between two well-endowed female Hispanic employees. I can't help but wonder what soft porn channel he manages to access at home.

It's now time for one of my inappropriate but popular jokes. I ask them, "Why don't chickens wear pants?" I see a look of blank stares facing me, common with groups of teenagers. I answer, "Because their peckers are on their heads." They all laugh loudly, and I remind them that what happens in the tenth grade boys' classroom stays in the tenth grade boys' classroom. I then use the remaining time to teach a lesson about forgiveness. I think to myself that I might need to garner some form of forgiveness for being accused of something I didn't do, but right now, I'm not feeling the warmth.

I pull out of the parking lot and head for home. I neglected to find out where my friends are going for lunch, but I don't feel like going anyway. I feel my mood turning blue as I park in the garage. My dogs greet me warmly, which makes them worth their trouble and expense. I change clothes and sit down to watch the Braves play a one o'clock game with the Mets. Probably due to my poor sleeping schedule of late, I fall asleep for three hours.

I wake up and hear the phone ringing, and I answer it without checking the caller ID. I'm still groggy but snap to alertness when I hear, "Mr. Harrington? This is Jim Kendall of the *Sentinel* calling you again. Sorry to bother you on Sunday. Can you speak for a minute?"

Mr. Todd's instructions to talk to no one about anything runs through my head, but I still answer, "Yes, I've got a few minutes." I'm too curious to hear what he has to say at this point.

Kendall then relates, "I'm calling because we plan to run a piece tomorrow about a local woman, Gayle Wade, who is accusing you of attempting to assault her sexually. Do you have any comments or a reply to this charge?"

My blood starts boiling and I think to myself that I have to maintain my composure. All I can manage to blurt out is, "Mister, there's not a word of truth to whatever she is saying about me."

He retorts, "She's alleging that you forced her into her bedroom and made her kiss you while you were trying to grope her. She said her boyfriend arrived at home in the nick of time and pulled you off of her."

I feel my brain go foggy as I try to process what this guy has just told me. Damn her, I thought to myself. The little voice in my head was instructing me to tell him I can't speak with him further on advice of my attorney, but I feel so wronged that I shout into the phone, "That's a bunch of garbage. She's a bald-faced liar!"

Kendall seems pleased with my explosive remark and asks, "Okay. Can I quote you on that?"

Losing what little composure I still had a tenuous grip on, I squeeze the phone hard and yell into it, "Gayle Wade, you and your lying rag of a paper can all go to hell!" I slam down the phone and throw it across the room. It hits the wall and breaks apart. I think to myself it's a good thing I have several cordless phones in the house and then I start to cry in frustration. I believe that my broken phone and my life are now in the same wretched condition.

Three hours later, I'm sitting in the same chair in the dark. I've prayed and considered who I can share my troubles with at this point. I wonder if I'll feel better if I can unload on someone. I haven't eaten in twelve hours but am not the least bit hungry. The dogs, who hid from me after I went nuclear with the phone, are whining to go outside. I let them out and back in before heading upstairs to my bedroom. I don't take out my contacts or remove my clothes; I just fall on the bed, and feeling both mad and sorry for myself, fall into a fitful sleep.

CHAPTER 12

MONDAY: SEVEN DAYS EARLIER

8:00 A.M.

The first thing I do after waking up is run two miles to get my blood flowing and clear my head. I return home, clean up, and get dressed. I eat some yogurt and fruit for breakfast. I know I need to call Mr. Todd quickly, and maybe Mr. Patterson in Birmingham. I dial the Houston legal office and leave an urgent message. Fifteen minutes later, he calls me back.

I tell him about my phone call yesterday with the *Sentinel* reporter. He doesn't get angry as I expected and says, "Well, it could have been worse. You didn't speak about any of the details of the field visit but generally denied her accusations, right?"

I answer, "That's right, but I also told him to go to the devil."

"Well, that's not the first time he's heard that in his line of work," Todd shared. "Again, I want you to promise me you won't talk to anybody about this matter and refer any and all contact to me or Mr. Patterson immediately. Are we clear on this?"

Feeling like I was caught with my hand in the cookie jar, I reply, "Yes, and I won't screw up again."

He shoots back, "I hope not. You can compromise your position with DPG if you're not more careful."

Hmm, a not-so-veiled threat, I think to myself, *but one I probably deserve.* "Putting my job at risk is the last thing I want to do," I tell him. "It's pretty much my life."

Todd then indicates, "You need to steel yourself for this whole deal to go public. I fully expect a story to appear in the *Sentinel,* and it will likely be picked up by the Atlanta paper and your local paper, if there is one."

In my mind's eye, I can see the local paper running a story on the front page; this is going to be brutal. Todd tells me he'll call Patterson and inform him of this latest development. He adds that I might expect a call from him. I thank him again, and we end the call.

Once again, my appetite seems to be on vacation, and I eat a light lunch. At 1:30 p.m., I check the *Sentinel* website. The story is on the third page of the electronic version of the paper. It reads,

GEORGIA MAN ACCUSED OF SEXUAL MISCONDUCT

A Helena woman and her attorney contacted police and charged a Disability Protection Group employee with inappropriate behavior of a sexual nature during an in-home interview that took place last Wednesday.

The Birmingham PD Sex Crimes Unit identified the alleged perpetrator as Mr. Kevin Harrington of Alpharetta, GA. Mr. Harrington is a field investigator for Disability Protection. Contact with their public relations department garnered no information other than confirmation that he is employed by the company. The police incident report indicates that a third person, Mr. Bob Ireland of Hoover, AL, is a friend of Ms. Wade and walked in on the alleged illegal act. The complaint indicates that Ms. Wade filed a claim for disability benefits with DPG.

Attempts to reach Mr. Harrington and Ms. Wade for comments were unsuccessful. A spokesperson for the Birmingham PD, Detective David Skirvin, acknowledged that an official complaint citing sexual abuse in the first degree was filed by Ms. Wade's attorney, Mr. Matthew Geary of the Geary Law Practice in Birmingham. When asked about the merits of a possible case against Mr. Harrington, Detective Skirvin would only state that he is "a person of interest, no more, no less." Disability Protection Group is a Texas–based company that sells disability policies and related products.

Well, the word is out. I feel as if I'm going to pass out as I read it over and over. I think the tone of the article makes me sound guilty, and it occurs to me that I've never before considered that a news article in print might be completely false. I hope, beyond hope, that this story stays on the back burner and doesn't reach the people I work with and know. I'm soon to find out that just the opposite is going to take place.

3:00 P.M.

I call Mr. Todd, and we briefly discuss the article. Per his request, I give him the web address of the online paper. I'm somewhat surprised that he still wants to keep my gag order in effect. I agree to it again, although I see little value in complying at this point. I momentarily wonder if Mr. Patterson is doing anything worthwhile on my behalf. I doubt it. For whatever reason, I have him pegged as a reactive lawyer, not one who will act before being poked and prodded.

Despite Mr. Todd's instructions, I feel I owe my mother the courtesy of being told what is going on with me. I call her and tell her about my dilemma. I write if off to her being eighty-eight that she keeps asking me to repeat myself, as if she can't process what I'm saying. She starts to cry, making me feel even worse.

I tell her not to discuss my situation with anyone, and she promises she won't. I have no doubt she'll keep her word, as she keeps things that she should share with me and others to herself. She says she is worried about me, and I reply that I am too. This initiates another bout of maternal sobbing, and I try to console her by saying everything will turn out fine. I wish I was confident this is actually true.

After extricating myself from this call, I sign onto my PC and Google for information about false sexual accusations. I find nothing I think is pertinent, but there are many stories about arrests, trials, and jail sentences. How comforting.

It's dinnertime, and I manage to eat most of a frozen dinner of baked salmon, broccoli, and mashed potatoes. I turn on the TV, hoping I don't end up being on the six o'clock local news. Thank goodness I'm not. I pace in my living room a good deal of the evening, not aware of what is on the TV. I like the white noise it's providing me. At about midnight, I've come to no conclusions about what I can do to improve my bleak situation. Unfortunately, it's soon to become bleaker.

CHAPTER 13

TUESDAY: SIX DAYS EARLIER

7:30 A.M.

I wake up to hear my work line ringing in my office down the hall from my bedroom. I jump out of bed, nearly trip over one of the dogs, and run to answer it. I don't make it but hear my voice message inviting the caller to leave a message. A few seconds, the blinking red light comes on at the base of the set, telling me a message was left.

I press the button, notice that my finger is shaking, and hear this: "Kevin, this is Buster Todd. I've got some not-so-good news to relate to you. Please call me as soon as you get this message." This sounds ominous to me. I trudge to the bathroom to relieve myself and splash some water on my hands and face. Replaying the message back in my office, I notice that Buster has left me a number that doesn't look familiar. It must be his direct line; more scary thoughts enter my head.

I call him back, and he answers on the second ring. "Buster Todd speaking."

I say in a shaky voice, "B-B-Buster, this is Kevin Harrington returning your call."

He hesitates a few seconds and then announces, "Kevin, I'm afraid I have some bad news for you. My boss and the vice president of human resources have decided that you are going to be placed on leave without pay pending the resolution of the charges filed against you. I want you to know that you are not being terminated, and you have the full protection of the Family Leave Medical Act for at least six weeks."

I'm stunned. I manage to ask, "When does my pay stop? I'm heavy into the 401K program and don't have a lot of other savings or cash on hand."

He replied, "You'll be paid through the end of this week. If you're on electronic funds transfer, the money will be in your checking account by the end of the day, Friday. I'm sorry this happened. The decision was made in conjunction with company policy and how similar employee situations have been handled in the past. I certainly hope this mess can be fixed quickly, and you can be reinstated."

This sounds like hollow conjecture to me. He then says, "Additionally, your PC access to the company employee website and the claim office will also be cut off in the next day or so."

I feel like I've been dropped off on a small desert island with a revolver to off myself. I plead with him, "Look, Buster.

Isn't there something else that can be done? I mean, I didn't do anything wrong. The only thing I would do different if I had it to do over again would be to call the cops and my boss after I left her house. I'm the victim here, don't you understand?"

Sounding noncommittal, he replies, "I'm really sorry, Kevin. It's actually out of my hands. Just to let you know, Mr. Patterson will be in touch with you when he needs to ask you anything. In the meantime, he's working diligently in your behalf." Somehow, I doubt this but say nothing.

I hesitate and ask, "Am I going to have to turn in my PC or my company cell phone?"

He replies, "I don't know if that has been discussed. Hang onto them right now, and let's let sleeping dogs lie." At least I can keep my cell phone for now. I've had a company cell for many years, and I cancelled our personal one when my wife died.

After an uncomfortable period of silence, I say, "Well, is that all? I guess I should get off the phone if you're done. By the way, are you my contact person? Is Mr. Patterson? Or do I have one now?"

He responds, sounding a little uncertain, "I'd say I still am. I'll call you if anything we need to discuss comes up. I wish you the best of luck. Good-bye, Kevin."

I sit stunned and think, *My God, nearly no job, no money, and accused of being a sexual deviant. What next?* Unfortunately, I don't have to wait too long to find out what's next.

11:30 A.M.

I haven't moved from my office chair since talking with Buster. I feel myself cramping and start to stand up when I hear my home phone ringing. My heart starts to race as I dash downstairs to get to the phone. I pick it up and say, "Hello." Funny, it doesn't sound like my own voice to me. Then I hear, "This is Detective Skirvin of the Birmingham Police. Is Kevin Harrington there?"

I tense up and reply, "This is he. I need to tell you that my company lawyer has told me not to speak to anyone about this mess that Wade woman has got me into."

He then says, "Look, Mr. Harrington, I don't have much to say to you other than to assure you we are looking at all angles of this case, including your background and Ms. Wade's background."

I feel slightly better when I recall all of the stuff I turned up trying to check out her disability claim. I state, "I'm not sure if I should say much without Mr. Patterson on the line. But I do want to let you know that this woman apparently has a record and is a huge liar."

Skirvin retorts, "You can trust that we know our business as far as conducting investigations, Mr. Harrington. I've tried to reach your attorney, Mr. Patterson, but he won't call me back. I felt I should let you know that we may need to speak with you in our offices in the next week or so. I left this same message with Mr. Patterson but wanted to be sure you are aware."

I tell him I'll keep this in mind, but he should go through Mr. Patterson for any future contact with me. I hesitate for a minute, thinking he sounds nice enough, and say, "Thanks for calling me, Detective Skirvin. I hope you get to the bottom of this and find the truth, which is that I did nothing wrong."

He remarks, "I'll keep that in mind. Thanks for your time."

After hanging up, I locate my notes from my first conversation with Buster and dial Patterson's number. I'm pretty upset at him for being short with me the only time we talked and, apparently, not calling the police back. Great, he doesn't answer. The call goes to his voice mail, and I note that he has recorded his own greeting. "This is the voice mail of Ken Patterson, attorney. Please leave your message at the beep." I briefly recount the details of my call with Detective Skirvin. I throw in a little dig and say that he, apparently, hasn't returned Skirvin's calls. Then I hang up.

I walk into the kitchen and sit down at the dining table. I've got so much to worry about now that I don't know where to begin. Bills that are due or soon will be cloud my sense of well-being. I'm caught in a vortex of uncertainty from a legal standpoint, and for the first time, I consider that if everything goes wrong, I might be jailed. Good God! And my reputation is bound to take a big hit. People might start thinking I'm some kind of deviant. I think about how my friends and I have joked about joining Pedophiles Anonymous, but now, it doesn't sound so funny.

I start crying again, and I feel ashamed of myself, thinking I'm not much of a man apparently. I remember my wife's health struggles and how brave she was in meeting her problems head-on. I figure she must be watching down on me and shaking her head in disgust at my poor reactions to an issue she would have gladly traded for if she could have recovered her health. I start to calm a little and tell myself that there's always hope, and I need to be as positive as possible so I don't jinx away a good outcome.

I look at the clock and see it's already 4:30 p.m. I've almost moped the day away. I decide to fix myself a cheeseburger and fries and then walk the dogs around the block. I do just that, and I'm even able to enjoy TV a little bit later in the evening. I'm interrupted at about 9:00 p.m. by a call from my mother who spends fifteen minutes crying and asking how something like this could happen to me. When I settle her down by lying that I know everything will turn our fine, I end the call. My mood ruined, I get ready to go to bed and lay my head on my pillow a little after 10:00 p.m. Mercifully, I quickly fall into a deep sleep.

CHAPTER 14

WEDNESDAY: FIVE DAYS EARLIER

I wake up at 8:00 a.m. and feel better than I have in a week. I know I have some massive troubles, but I keep thinking that other people are worse off than I am. Thinking about this a little more, I have trouble identifying too many such persons beyond those with terminal diseases or the guys sitting on death row in prison. I try to move on to happier thoughts.

I rethink the fact that I've not spoken about my troubles with anyone except my mother, the least likely one to handle it well. I decide I need to call my kids today and a few close friends. The heck with Buster Todd and his gag order; he seems to have abandoned ship on me anyway.

Despite my soon-to-be-dire financial situation, I decide to take my work clothes to the cleaner's. Maybe this little positive gesture that I might need clean work duds will work some good karma for me somehow. Plus, I'll have no deadline on picking them up.

Anyway, I look forward to visiting with the owner of the cleaners who is a Korean transplant that speaks in broken English. A former Asian Tour and Nike Tour golfer, he gave me ten golf lessons about six months ago for $300. I like to tell him that, despite his instruction, I'm a "handicapped" golfer with a handicap that can only be determined with a calculator. He laughs at this heartily, but I think the language barrier gets in the way a little.

I enter Super Cleaners and hand my bag of clothes to K.J. Chin, the owner and my golf instructor. We banter for a few minutes and agree to schedule a round of golf at some time in the future when his teaching schedule lessens. I leave and admire the 2011 black Mercedes E350 parked across the parking lot. During my lessons a few months ago, he shared that he bought the car with winnings from two Nike Tour events he won a couple of years ago.

I drive home and call my kids. My son is in Milwaukee on business, and I explain what happened to him. He listens and then expresses his concern for me. He says he is concerned about the Birmingham lawyer, Patterson, based on what I told him. I reply that I'm concerned about him and his apparent lack of efforts too. My son then suggests I speak with the pastor of my church. I promise to consider this idea.

Next, I call my daughter in Lubbock, Texas, who is pursuing a PhD in theater. She is between classes and listens to my brief summary of what has happened. She is very concerned, and I can tell she is near tears.

She asks me if I want to use my airline frequent flyer points to get her a plane ticket to come home and support me. I tell her there's really nothing she can do here, and she should stay at Texas Tech. I am humbled by her offer to drop everything in the face of her demanding schedule, which includes a full fifteen-hour course load and teaching a freshman drama class.

I leash my dogs and take them for a late morning walk. I'm gone for about forty-five minutes and feel a little better, although I don't know how I'll make it financially if this thing drags out for more than a few weeks. When I walk through the front door, I see my phone message blinking. I feel a slight wave of panic and hope I don't have to endure any more bad news. There are two messages, and the first one is a shock.

I press the button and hear, "Kevin, this is Scott at the church. Please call me as soon as you get this message." Scott is the youth minister at Third Baptist Church, and I have the uneasy feeling that he isn't calling to tell me what a great job I'm doing with the tenth grade boys. I briefly wonder if he caught wind of the joke I told last Sunday. If so, I'll owe an apology for it. As it turns out, it's not about the questionable joke.

The church receptionist connects me to Scott, and he begins, "Thanks for calling back so quick, Kevin."

"I haven't discussed this with anyone, but I'm off work for a little while, so I got your message pretty quickly," I admit while I drum my fingers on the table.

He then says, "Kevin, I'm not real PC- and Internet-knowledgeable as you probably know. But I usually read the Atlanta paper and the Alpharetta paper online each day before they're delivered to my house the next morning. I saw a very disturbing story about you in both papers today. I want you to know that I'm here to support you and so are the pastor and the rest of the church staff."

I'm taken aback by this—partially because I don't know exactly what is in the articles he read. I answer, "Scott, I was told to refrain discussing this with others, but I can assure you that I did nothing wrong and expect to be fully cleared of any charges filed. I appreciate your offer of support, and I was thinking about calling the pastor to schedule an appointment with him to discuss things."

Scott then tells me, "Buddy, I believe in you, but unfortunately, the congregation may not be as understanding. I have to assume that this story will be seen or heard by most of them. I have to answer to the parents of our students, and I'm anticipating some negative feedback from them, especially the parents of the boys in your class. I discussed this with the pastor, and we came to the conclusion that, until your legal troubles are cleared up, you can't teach."

I'm stunned and feel as if I've been slapped in the face. Deep down inside, I understand Scott's position, but it still stings. Due to today's legal climate, the church requires all Sunday school teachers to pass an annual background check. This is probably to be sure there are no known pedophiles trying to get close to the kids. But I'm being considered guilty until proven innocent—and by the church, no less! I angrily think my prayers are obviously going unanswered.

Weakly, Scott then adds, "We're here for you, pal. Let us know if we can do anything to help."

I think I detect a hint of insincerity in his voice and reply, "Sure, if I need any more positive backing, I'll call you." It's a little edgy, but saying this makes me feel a little better. I hear Scott start to say something else, and I hang up on him. I throw the phone on the floor and begin pacing.

Almost immediately, the phone rings again, and I pick it up. The caller ID indicates a church number, and I let it ring. I don't trust myself to speak rationally right now, so I decide it's better to not tighten the imaginary noose around my neck any more. I note that Scott, assuming he was the caller, leaves no message.

I bang my finger down on the still blinking message light and brace myself for more "sunshine." It's from Patterson, my so-called Alabama attorney. He simply says, "Mr. Harrington, call me today if possible." He then leaves his phone number. I dial him and am placed on hold for ten minutes. Big surprise.

He finally comes on the line and asks, "How're you doing, Mr. Harrington?" I tell him I've had better days and that the local media is apparently picking up the story now. He responds, "That's exactly what Ms Wade and her attorney want. If things get hot for you and Disability Protection Group, they believe a generous settlement will be more likely."

I ask him if he got my message about hearing from the police, and he replies, "Yes, I did. Understand that I haven't returned their call purposely. I don't think they plan to arrest you anytime soon, and I want them to go ahead and investigate Ms. Wade and her history. I have your notes and taped statements, and as you found out, her background is checkered at best."

Hearing him say this gives me a small sense of relief until he follows up with, "But they will have to consider that she may be telling the truth despite the fact she hasn't been a model citizen in the past." There goes my minor relief down the drain.

I disagree, "But her whole story is bull. It's all based on her lies, and the boyfriend is lying through his teeth too if he says I was putting the moves on her."

Patterson replies, "I hear you, but the fact is she does have a witness, be he truthful or not. Based on your version of what happened, she may have planted a kiss on you for DNA purposes. I don't know if a lab team was sent to her house or not, but I did learn that she probably called the cops right after you walked out the door."

Man, I think to myself. I made such a huge error when I didn't call the cops or my boss when I should have but no sense bringing that up to this guy.

Patterson continues, "I'm not sure where the police are going with this. It's not beyond the realm of possibility that they ask you to come into the station for an interview and a DNA sample."

After a few seconds of uncomfortable silence, I ask, "So our best option now is to sit back and see what the police do?"

He replies, "Yes. I know you don't want to hear that, but we are best served by staying in a reactive mode. If we're lucky, we may have to do little or nothing depending on their assessment of the plaintiff's case. It's still most likely that she and the boyfriend are looking for a settlement and not a day in court."

"And in the meantime," I retort, "I have to deal with false accusations that ruin my reputation?"

Patterson responds, "I'm afraid there's nothing to done about that. It's the way the system is." This answer doesn't make me feel any better. He then tries to close the call with,

"I'll contact you immediately when something comes up that requires we do something."

I ask, "Can this thing go on for weeks and weeks?"

After a few seconds, he says, "Maybe."

Man, what a great legal mind, I think. I don't bother saying good-bye and hang up. I don't remember ever hanging up on anyone since I was a teenager making crank calls. This makes twice in one day; maybe I should start keeping track and see how many people I can do it to.

I look at the clock and note it is nearly 2:00 p.m. The day is flying by, and I wish it were over so nothing else bad can transpire. My dogs are barking at the front picture window, which is unusual, so I walk into the living room to see what has their attention. I'm not surprised to see my neighborhood female admirer walking her little white dog. I hope she's not bringing me more food and another unspoken visual invitation.

I do a double take when I see what is going on. She appears to be leading her dog into my yard and encouraging it to take a dump. I crack open the front door and hear her say, "Come on, baby. Go poo poo." I keep my yard nicely manicured, and I take plastic bags with me when walking my dogs so I can clean up any messes they make. I find it somewhat humorous—but at the same time, irritating—that she is coaxing her pooch to make a deposit on my front lawn.

I open the door and say, "How're you and your dog doing today?"

I'm taken aback by the hateful look she gives me before saying, "Don't talk to me, you pervert."

I respond, "At least I don't try to line my neighbors' yards with fresh manure."

She yells out, "You leave me alone or I'll call the police."

Wow, I think, *word on me is getting around*. I then say to her, "It'll be a lot easier to leave you alone if you and your dog stay out of my yard." She glares at me again, tugs on her mutt's leash and huffs off down the street.

I close my front door and, since I'm apparently now a known sexual deviant, lock it. I sit on my couch and reflect on how poorly this day is going. My mother is elderly, lives out of state, and would only stare at me if she were here. I can't drag my kids from their lives to come to Georgia for who knows how long, and more importantly, what could they do if they were here?

For what seems to be developing into an hourly event, I put my head in my hands and weep softly at my situation. Damn that Wade woman. I wish she would fall off of a cliff, and I surmise, I wouldn't mind helping her start such a journey with a firm shove. I reflect sadly that I'm now envisioning myself hurting or even killing someone. How noble of me.

I sit on my couch feeling sorry for myself for a long time, thinking about nothing in particular but recalling isolated events. I reminisce about happy times in my life and am surprised at what pops into my mind. I remember all of the times I was injured in my twenties while playing softball and engaging in other sports. My mind drifts back to waterskiing without my contacts and barreling into a buoy at a lake.

I also go over the time when I took one more swing on a vine after my kids and their friends were done. Of course, when I was at the apex of an arc about thirty feet over a dried out creek bed, the vine broke. I fell on a rock hidden under a lot of leaves and broke a leg. My wife, being used to my injury-prone lifestyle, calmly told me to lie still while she went to look for a wheelchair and a park ranger. Leave it to Linda to stay in control and take care of things.

A short time later, I had another skiing accident just before sunset. Skiing with my contacts this time, I misjudged my distance from the shore and did a slingshot maneuver to look cool and glide up to land's edge. Instead, I hit land going full speed and ran into a large downed tree trunk. I landed on the back of my head and neck but not before losing a ski and having it strike an innocent bystander, bruising her liver. Witnessing his father nearly kill himself, my then five-year-old son proceeded to ask his mother, "Mom, why didn't you move that tree so Dad wouldn't hit it?" He was learning to spread the blame at an early age.

I catch myself smiling as I think about another unrelated event in college. I briefly wonder if I'm going just a little crazy to think about past experiences at a time like this. I again let my mind wander and find myself in college in the mid-seventies. I played NAIA baseball for one season and was a seldom-used pitcher and outfielder. But I feel myself grinning again as I recall some great times during my freshman year in my fraternity, Kappa Delta Rho.

This was the era of unrestricted hazing and frat house pledges everywhere had to go through "hell week" before being initiated into the chapters as active members. I was briefly the "rock star" of the pledge class as a result of one of the many tests we were subjected to during this nearly sleepless and demanding week.

I remember it like it happened yesterday. The windows of the dining room were lined with newspapers, and me and my eight fellow pledge-mates were asked to line up on one end of the room. We noticed a large tin tub of ice in the middle of the room. We were then ordered to strip down to our birthday suits, not the first time this week we'd been asked to go totally or partially nude.

We were then given the rules of this exercise. One of the senior members of the fraternity explained that a cherry would be placed on top of the ice and we would each have one chance to pick it up. The kicker was that we couldn't use any part of our bodies to do so other than our butt cheeks. How cosmopolitan.

Somehow, I was the last one to make the attempt. The other pledges had all shuffled up to the tub of ice with looks of shame on their faces. The active brothers were fairly juiced up on beer and yelling all sorts of demeaning and derogatory things as each pledge made halfhearted attempts to pick the cherry. Then it was my turn.

Thankfully, a fresh cherry was placed on the ice for each participant. I had been thinking about what to do while watching the almost sad machinations of my fellow exhibitionists. I walked around the tub several times as if reviewing it from every angle. I then knelt down from different angles around the tub and stared past my upraised thumb, much the same way a golfer does before taking an important putt.

At this point, with a totally serious facial expression, I marched up to the tub and straddled it so the cherry was directly beneath me and my lower anatomy. I shook my arms and hands as if I was limbering them up and quickly swooped downward until I felt the ice on my cheeks. I immediately stood back up and was astonished that the cherry was no longer visible. Obviously, there was only one place it could be.

After a few seconds of silence, the room erupted into a chorus of clapping, shouting, and hooting. I received hearty handshakes and was backslapped by all of the active brothers, many of whom told me something like they had no idea I was so gifted asswise. When I squatted downward, releasing the pressure between my cheeks, the cherry fell out. It was retrieved with a napkin and disposed of before someone thought of making it a dessert for me or one of the other pledges.

It was a brief shining moment of glory during my freshman year of college. And facing daunting legal issues and probable character assassination in 2013 in my living room, the memories allow me to experience a brief touch of relief from my problems. This will prove to be the last respite for me. From here on out, things will quickly spiral more and more out of control.

CHAPTER 15

THURSDAY: FOUR DAYS EARLIER

I wake up in the morning, and the first thing that comes to my mind is the Atlanta and Alpharetta newspapers are now delivered to driveways and mailboxes throughout the area. My vilification is about to expand exponentially. I decide to stay in the house all day and, hopefully, let some of the dust settle. I hear my doorbell ring at midmorning, and I hesitate to answer it.

I glance through the peephole and see it's Joan; I can't recall her last name but know she's the president of the neighborhood association. I slowly open the door and ask her what's up. With a sneer on her face, she says, "You're breaking homeowner association rules by not keeping your garage door in acceptable condition." I tell her I have no idea what she's talking about, and she invites me to come outside and take a look.

I'm shocked to see two words that look as if they were hurriedly spray painted in black on my bright white double garage door—*rapist* and *pervart*. Unable to resist, I ask her, "Are you a good speller?"

She sees no humor in my question and states adamantly, "You have twenty-four hours to get that off of your door, or you'll be subject to a fine from the homeowners' association."

I reply, "Joan, surely you realize I didn't put those words on my own door. I'll remove them or paint over them as soon as possible. You have any idea who might have done this?"

She replied, "How in the world would I know that?" before pivoting and marching down my driveway to a waiting car.

I see a male driver waiting for her. Probably her husband, I figure. I guess she decided she might need some backup to visit me. I walk back into my house, and for the first time, I feel the beginning of a burning rage forming in the back of my mind. Like I don't have enough trouble without some mental midget deciding to decorate my house.

I feel like venting to someone, so I call my neighbor and friend, Noel. Although he's at work, he usually answers his cell when I call him. He picks up on the second ring and says, "Hello."

I think I notice a tone of resignation in his voice. "Noel," I say, "how are you?"

He replies, "Okay." Again, a one word response; it's not like him.

I begin, "I've been meaning to talk with you, but I've been busy. I had some trouble this morning. Some dirtbag spray painted some slurs on my garage door."

He says, "Oh."

Now, my radar is buzzing. This isn't like the Noel I'm friends with; he's an avid talker on nearly any subject. Going on the defensive, I decide to find out if he thinks I'm a criminal like at least one other person in the neighborhood does. "Have you seen today's paper?" I inquire.

He says, "Yes."

This is ridiculous I think to myself and blurt out, "You don't believe the garbage being printed about me, do you?" And of all things, there is no reply. I check my cell screen and confirm we're still connected. Starting to see red a little, I state loudly, "Thanks for your support in my time of need, buddy. Talk to you when hell freezes over!"

I break the connection and toss my phone on the floor. I'm starting to feel isolated, but weirdly enough, I feel good about giving Noel a little guff. Maybe I'm looking at this thing the wrong way, I ponder. Maybe I need to go on the offensive a little since no one seems to be in my corner.

As I back out of my garage to go to the hardware store for some paint, I see both the local paper and the Atlanta papers in the driveway. I pick them up and glance through them. The Atlanta paper has a blurb about me buried in the Metro Section, not real noticeable. But the Alpharetta paper, which publishes on Sundays, Mondays, Thursdays, and Fridays, put me on the front page of today's edition. The headline reads LOCAL MAN ACCUSED OF ASSAULT. The byline source is identified as the Associated Press, and the article is pretty much verbatim to the Birmingham papers of yesterday. Thank God no one printed a picture of me.

I drive to Ace Hardware and feel a slow burn beginning in the back of my head. I'm getting frustrated and irritable at my seemingly hopeless situation. A guy in front of me doesn't notice the light is green, and I blast my horn at him. He gives me the one finger salute and slowly accelerates. I tailgate him real close for a couple of blocks before backing off. It isn't like me to do something bordering on road rage, but it gives me a small flush of satisfaction. At least that jerk did a little something I could react to.

I walk into Ace and feel like all eyes in the store are on me. I ask a clerk what would be the best to remove some graffiti from a white garage door. He asks if I have a problem, and this offends me. I say to him, "Maybe. Do you have a problem?" The young man blushes and says he will get the manager to help me. "Fine," I say loudly.

A middle-aged man approaches and says to me, "Is there a problem, sir?"

I lose my temper and say loudly, "Why? Are you people psychologists?"

Mr. Merkle, per the name tag on his shirt, replies, "We don't want any trouble." Unfortunately, I say the first wisecrack that comes into my head, "Neither did George Custer." I grin at Mr. Merkle, proud of my quick wit.

He looks at the clerk I had just intimidated and says, "Call them."

I wasn't born yesterday and decide that they are most likely calling the police. I cool down quickly and realize that the last thing I need to happen now is some kind of confrontation with the law. I have enough to worry about. Without a word to any of the hardware staff, I march to the front door, jump in my car, and drive away. Two blocks down the road, I see a cop car speeding in the direction I had just come from. I hope no one saw my car, or worse, got my license plate.

I drive aimlessly for about fifteen minutes and think about what just took place. At first, I'm ashamed of my behavior. I also think about Ms. Wade's lies about me, which also makes me feel ashamed. I say to myself, "Knock it off. You did nothing wrong. Don't be a wimp and feel sorry for yourself or embarrassed. You're in the right."

My mood seems to be swinging wildly from near euphoria to extreme sadness. One minute I'm confident that by telling the truth, I will prevail and be exonerated. But the next minute, I feel like the cards are stacked against me, and the truth doesn't matter. Now I'm getting another headache.

I pull off of the road for a little while and hope the pain in my temple will subside. I lean back in my seat and close my eyes. I'm in the parking lot of a Walmart, so I shouldn't be disturbed amidst all of the cars. I drift off and nap for almost an hour. I wake and feel somewhat better, but I still feel the weight of the world on my shoulders. At least my headache is gone.

I decide I'll stay under the radar this time and not cause any waves. I surmise that the best way to do this is to have no contact with anyone if possible. I go into the Walmart and an employee asks if she can help me. Ignoring her, I look straight ahead and keep walking. In some strange way, this makes me feel good.

I find the paint section and select a gallon of exterior white semi-gloss paint as well as two brushes. I pay the cashier almost $25 with my debit card and recall that my salary will cease shortly, making even minor shopping trips like this one tough. I drive back home and avoid any conflicts with other drivers. I paint over the words on my door, applying two coats. Noticing that the area painted over is brighter than the rest of the door, I repaint the entire door. As I finish in the late afternoon, I am pleased with the result. Also, I realize I killed a few hours engaging in physical activity that effectively prevented me from brooding over my circumstances.

It's now early evening, and after showering and putting on some clean clothes, I put a pizza in the oven and turn on the local news. I wait for the sports to begin when the floor drops out from under me. I see a still picture of someone who looks eerily like me when the news channel talking head says, "And a report coming out of Birmingham indicates that an Alpharetta man is facing charges of sexual assault during a visit to a woman's home in Helena, Alabama, a few miles south of Birmingham. Kevin Harrington of Alpharetta has been accused of trying to fondle Gayle Wade during an interview in connection with her claim for disability with Mr. Harrington's employer, Disability Protection Group of Houston. The man on your screen is Mr. Harrington, pictured in his church directory. We caught up with Ms. Wade's attorney, Mr. Matthew Geary of the Geary Law Practice in Birmingham."

I'm frozen to the screen as Geary is shown speaking to the camera. "My client filed a claim for disability benefits, and Disability Protection Group sent Mr. Harrington to interview her even though she submitted what I believe is solid proof of her injury. I can't go into details now of what happened other than to say Mr. Harrington obviously acted improperly toward my client. We're waiting for the Birmingham police to take appropriate action in this matter."

I feel my knees shaking as the newscaster continues, "We called Disability Protection, but their public relations person would not confirm or deny anything other than Mr. Harrington is one of their employees. Action News will bring you more on this story as it develops over the next several days. Now, for the sports..."

I'm feel numb and don't know what to do. My phone rings, and I answer it, not checking the caller ID. "Hey scumbag, think you can do anything you want because you work for a big insurance company? I know where you live and—" I don't hear any more as I slam the phone down. The phone starts ringing off the hook over the next thirty minutes, and I finally disconnect it at the phone jack. The pizza burns before I remember to take it out of the oven. I notice that the oven timer is ringing when I turn off the heat and throw the burnt food in the trash can.

I can't believe this is happening to me. I drink a Coke and eat some plain white bread just to get something in my stomach. I hear something in the street and fear that some more neighbor mischief may be brewing. I turn off all of my lights and turn off the TV. I take the dogs to the backyard to use the restroom. Thankfully, no one sees me.

I figure I can watch TV in the basement without giving away the fact I'm home. I go through the house and close all of the blinds. I then sit in the dark in my living room. My mother calls my cell phone, and I don't answer it. I know it'll worry her, but I don't know what to say to her right now. I think that I will need to phone her tomorrow, or she may send someone to look for me. Thankfully, my kids don't call—or at least, don't try—my cell. I get a text from Noel that reads, "Hang in there." I'm not sure how to respond so I don't.

I sit on my couch and think I'm falling apart, both physically and mentally. I notice tremors in my hands, and I can't remember what type of car I own. I think that this is crazy and very frightening. I see no way out of my dilemma because the truth doesn't seem to carry any weight. Thoughts are racing through my head—some of them inconsequential, such as the short dress a girl I dated once in college wore.

I go into the bathroom after midnight to brush my teeth and turn the light on. Immediately, I turn it off for fear of giving a sign that I'm home. In doing so, I drop the toothpaste and bang my forehead on the sink leaning down to pick it up in the dark. I lose my temper and throw my electric toothbrush in the direction of the mirror. I hear the mirror break and feel some glass hit me in the face.

I breathe deeply in an attempt to calm myself. Finding the toothbrush and toothpaste, I go to the half bath on the first floor and close the door. Since there are no exterior windows in the powder bath, I turn on the lights and brush my teeth. I then splash some water on my face and start crying. I wish that my wife were still alive to be with me tonight. She always had a way of dealing with anything that might come up.

Thinking about Linda makes me ashamed of myself again. "Come on," I tell myself, "Linda handled tougher problems than this." Then I come to the realization that maybe she didn't. Her health issues didn't involve people believing, or at least, being told, bad things about her. I think to myself that I'm truly in a no-win situation. My life is simply out of my hands, I realize, and I've never felt so helpless with nowhere to turn.

I curl up on the cool wooden floor of the hallway and think to myself, *What am I going to do? I wish I could get away from everything.* That is my last thought as I pass out on the floor, dropping into an uneasy state of sleepy exhaustion.

CHAPTER 16

FRIDAY: THREE DAYS EARLIER

I wake up with a stiff neck, probably because I have no pillow, and my head is rammed up against the wall. I get up and check my watch. Wow, it's one in the afternoon. I've slept for over twelve hours. Like a wet blanket, all of my worries again begin to weigh down on me. I go right into the bathroom and experience a loose stool, which seems incredible since I've eaten so little over the past several days.

I shower, change clothes, and look out into the front yard. No angry mobs or burning crosses, I guess that's a little positive. I see the paper in the driveway and decide to get it later. I don't feel like reading it anyway. I ponder whether or not to call the Net Insurance attorney or the clown in Birmingham. I decide not to since they know how to reach me. Plus, I don't really want to talk with them, or anyone else for that matter.

I make myself a bologna sandwich and think to myself, *What in the world can I do?* I now see how people can be driven to harming or even killing themselves. I always thought of suicide as indicative of someone with a mental problem or being a weak person. Now I'm not so sure, but this doesn't seem like a viable option for me in any way, shape, or form.

Who can I look to for help? Of all people to come to mind, I recall my dad. He died about ten years ago at age seventy -seven and had multiple health issues. You have to give him one thing though. He was super confident. The man never made a mistake; he would confirm this resolutely. He also had issues with alcohol, which is probably the main reason I've never taken up drinking, socially or otherwise.

But dad was super smart, even though he didn't have the opportunity to put his smarts to much use. He went to college for two years, working his way through by earning tuition money as a kitchen worker in a sorority. He had an opportunity to go to work for the post office at age twenty and took it. He married my mother a year later, and I came along about three years afterward. When I was eleven years old, my parents adopted a one-year-old boy.

At five ten, I'm the tallest one on my mom's or dad's side of the family. My adopted brother, Nick, grew up to be six two and two hundred pounds of muscle. My brother and I both played high school football, but my best sport was baseball while he was a true track star. I remember my dad instructing me, and later, my brother about competing in sports, and in his way, life.

He told me to act like I've been there before when I cross the goal line for a touchdown. He also gave that sage advice to my brother, although we both had very few chances to put this approach in practice. Dad also said that a person needs to fight and claw and take what he can get from life. I always thought this was amusing because he didn't practice this mantra unless heavy drinking was his goal.

However, he said something over and over to me and Nick which I never forgot. I can hear him saying it even now in his deep, harsh, alcohol-fueled voice, "Never back away from anything, never. Fight for yourself, and when you're exhausted, fight some more. Take care of yourself and the hell with everyone else. You can't count on anyone but yourself. It's okay if people are a little afraid of you. That means you're a winner and someone to be reckoned with."

Although I didn't think he practiced this all the time in his life, he did in most cases. He was as mean as a junkyard dog in a fight despite being only 5'7" and 180 pounds. Also, he chose only one path when he thought someone had wronged him—confrontation.

As I finish up my lunch, I think of what my dad would have done in my situation. I grin as I envision him going to the Wade house and facing her and her boyfriend down with threats that he was more than willing to back up. Yes, I think he would have kicked ass and taken names later.

In the past, I always thought he was old-school and, to a fault, prone to engaging in conflicts with others at the drop of a hat. However, right now, his approach doesn't sound so bad since my more conservative courses of action are panning out to be as worthless as my two do-nothing attorneys.

After cleaning up my lunch dishes, I walk through my yard and check the front and back of the house for any signs of vandalism or additional misspelled messages in painted form. All seems fine. I go back into the house, sit back down at the table, and reminisce about another time I saw my dad and his take-no-prisoners approach in action. This incident took place when I was thirteen years old and of considerable talent in the local junior baseball league made up of thirteen-, fourteen-, and fifteen-year-old boys.

I was only thirteen but a star in the league. One of my good friends, Tom Lady, was also playing; he was a pitcher and shortstop while I played outfield and hit for power. Our coach, Jerry Hanover, had a son playing too. He was small in stature and played second base. A decent athlete, he was not at the same level as me and my friend. At the end of the summer, the coaches of the six teams in our league selected four boys to play in the city all-star game at Turner Field.

My buddy and I were told by Coach Hanover that we were selected to participate. We were both pumped about it and looked forward to being involved. What we didn't know was that Coach Hanover was notified of a specific date to report for all-star practice with the players picked from around the Atlanta area. He didn't tell me or Tom of the practice dates, and therefore, we missed the first two and were cut.

We learned what happened and understood why Coach Hanover did this when an article in the Atlanta paper listed the junior baseball league all-star team members. Coach Hanover's son and a player from another team in our league were listed as replacement players for two kids who made the team but were no-shows.

I was furious, and so was Tom. Strangely enough, my dad seemed relatively calm, even though he pieced together what had happened before I did. A couple of days later, on a Friday afternoon, Dad told me to get in the car so we could return my uniform to Coach Hanover. I noticed a crooked grin on his face, and I thought it could be an interesting trip.

We pulled up to Coach Hanover's house, and my dad walked quickly up the sidewalk to the front door. Mrs. Hanover answered the bell, and dad said in a polite and respectful voice, "Is Coach Hanover in?"

She smiled and replied, "Sure, Mr. Harrington, let me get him for you." I thought to myself, *She's clueless as to the fireworks that are about to go off on her front porch.*

The coach walked to the door but kept the screen door closed. He said to dad, "Hi. What can I do for you guys?"

My dad stated, "We know what shenanigans you pulled with Kevin and Tom so your boy could play on the all-star team. I'd like you to step out here on your front porch so I can shove this uniform where the sun doesn't shine." I was almost disappointed that he didn't use any cuss words.

I saw Coach Hanover look my dad in the eye, and even though he was about 6'3" and 230 pounds, he sensed a valid threat and simply closed and bolted the front door.

My dad looked at me and said, "That's too damn bad. Here, hand me the uniform." He placed it between the doors and slammed the screen door so hard, I thought it would come off of its hinges. He then yelled out, "I hope to run into you sometime, Coach, real hard!" Then he turned to me and said in an almost reverent voice, "Well, I guess we're done here. Let's go home, son."

Dad was sort of a folk hero to my friends after this incident, the details of which spread far and wide in no small part due to my retelling of it to everyone I knew. Although I knew deep inside that there might have been a better, more mature way to have handled this situation, I felt good that my dad was willing to stand up for me. And now I start to think that maybe I should stand up for myself in my dismal situation. *But how?* I wonder.

It's getting to be late afternoon before I realize my home phone is still disconnected from the wall jack. I decide I'll leave it like that for the time being. I get a legal-sized pad of paper and proceed to write down all of my issues I'm facing at present. I think this will help me sort things out and maybe come up with a reasonable course of action.

I draw a line vertically down the middle of the page and mark a + on one side and a – on the other side. I start on the positive side but can't think of anything to list besides my mother and kids being willing to support me. I guess that's better than nothing, but I'm disappointed that I really can't think of anything else to put down. I note in parenthesis behind this sole entry that I want to keep them out of my problems due to my mom's age and the busy schedules of my kids. Besides, I think to myself, what can they really do to help?

Now, it's time to list the not-so-good details of my situation. This side of the ledger dwarfs the positive side in a short time as I begin to list my immediate problems—harm to my reputation, property vandalism, anxious mental state, no clear solution, possible loss of job, loss of income, lousy attorneys, general assumption that I'm guilty, being targeted by others who have little or no knowledge of the facts, trouble sleeping, feeling despair to the point I feel overwhelmed and cry, self-doubt, irritability and loss of temper, and the possibility I could face punishment even though I'm innocent.

Man, what a list. At this time, my cell phone rings, and I don't recognize the number. I hesitate before answering it, "Hello?"

I hear, "Hi, Kevin. This is Pastor Day. I've been trying to call you, but your number doesn't seem to be working. I'm glad I had your cell number. Got a minute?" I tell him I have plenty of time, and he proceeds, "We've all heard about the accusations against you. How're you holding up?" I lie and say I'm doing good, considering.

He continues, "The entire church is concerned about you, and I'm praying for you daily." I say nothing, and he asks, "Is there anything we can do for you?"

I respond, "I don't know how to answer that, Pastor. I feel lost and abandoned. You're the first person I've heard from that didn't want to criticize me or threaten me."

Pastor Day countered, "Don't lose hope, Kevin." *Too late for that*, I thought. He continued, "I believe you'll be exonerated soon."

I tell him thanks, and then he drops a bombshell. "Kevin," he begins, "the deacons met this afternoon and made a difficult decision. Your church membership is apparently public knowledge to the news media. We were told by two local TV stations that they plan to have camera crews on-site this Sunday morning in case you attend services. They also said they plan to interview you and some of the members in attendance if you're at the service. I don't think you did those things that woman is accusing you of, but we think it will hurt the church to be associated with you right now."

I can't believe my ears. My church is ashamed of me?

"I want you to know," Pastor Day continues, "that we plan to issue a public statement supporting you as soon as your legal issues are cleared up. Do you understand the church's position, Kevin? We depend on our offering revenue, and this could put a real damper on things for us."

If I felt down before, now I'm crushed. It takes all of my strength to say to him, "Yes, I understand. Thanks for the call." Then, before he can say anything else, I end the call.

I can't believe what I just heard. I feel like crying, but I'm too shocked. My life seems to be spiraling out of control, and a big area of support I thought I could count on is no longer a viable option. *Those damn deacons*, I think. *How many of them have done things even worse than what I'm falsely accused of doing?*

It's at this very moment I decide to change my approach to everything. From now on, I'm going to fight and be someone to be reckoned with. I'm going to take care of myself and the hell with everyone else. I feel myself grimace, grin, and say to myself, *Look out, world!*

CHAPTER 17

SATURDAY: TWO DAYS EARLIER

I actually have a restful night of sleep and wake up feeling better than I have in the last four to five days. I realize I'm feeling better because I'm in attack mode now. I'm going to come up with something constructive to do in my own best interests. Someone is going to pay for my injustices, and the number one candidate is Gayle Wade. I determine that I need to make a detailed plan of action and not be disturbed by anyone while doing so.

I decide that being at home is not a good idea. The whole town seems to be against me, and I need to have some space and not have to worry about vandalism or more potshots like the one Pastor Day laid on me. Therefore, after taking my dogs outside and feeding them, I load them into my car. I'll be better off boarding them for a few days while I decide what I need to do.

I take them to a Marietta, Georgia, animal boarding facility I find on the Internet, and thankfully, there is room for them.

I tell them my name is Joe Smith and give my home number, which won't receive calls until I reconnect my phone. I pay cash in advance for three days of standard care, and though they seem surprised I'm paying up front, they accept the money and tell me not to worry about my dogs. I think to myself, *I won't. I've got bigger fish to fry.*

I go home and sign on to my online bank accounts. I transfer $500 from my savings to my checking account and drive to an ATM to take out the same amount. Now I have money to formalize my plan and put it into action. I determine that I have to be under the radar to accomplish whatever I decide to put in play. I access the Internet and look for a place to spend the night and work on a plan with no one bothering me or being aware of my whereabouts.

I find Rock Island State Park in Rock Island, Tennessee. It's a little less than two hundred miles to the north and will take about three and a half hours to get there. Importantly, it's between Nashville and Knoxville in an isolated part of the state. I reach the park reservation office and inquire about renting one of their A-frame cabins for one night only. The clerk tells me that someone didn't show up and a unit is available until Monday morning.

I rent the unit for tonight and tell the clerk I'll pay cash when I arrive. He wants a credit card over the phone, and I tell him I don't use them. He warns me that if someone with a valid credit card calls, he'll have to give them the unit instead. I don't think this is likely due to the out-of-the-way location of the park and tell the clerk I'll take my chances. I also tell him my name is Jack Bobo. If anyone tries to follow me when

I leave home, I think they'll give up after a while. Plus, I can watch for any cars that remain in my rearview mirror for too long. So far, so good, I think to myself.

Although I don't know exactly what I'm going to do yet, I decide I may need a gun for persuasion purposes. I tell myself I don't have to load it if I don't want to, but I better have one available for appearance's sake. I'm in good shape in this area because I already own one. My daughter divorced her former husband a couple of years ago. He worked out of the country about ten months out of the year and wanted her to have a gun for protection.

Although she took one lesson from the husband of a friend at a shooting range, she never warmed to the idea of being a gun owner. Shortly after the divorce was final, she asked me if I wanted the gun. She had never bothered to register it, and I didn't do so after she gave it to me. Effectively, I had a gun that is not listed in any state or national gun owner's registry. It takes me less than forty-five minutes to file off the manufacturer's registration number of my .22 caliber Beretta. I fired it 20–25 times at a shooting range with a friend a few months ago. I have two boxes of hollow-point shells courtesy of my daughter.

It was late morning, and I left for Tennessee. I wanted to be there by midafternoon so I had plenty of time to be by myself and to think and plan. I smile as I realize I'll be completely out of the loop and isolated from everyone. This will give me the chance to come up with something that would make my dad proud. The little voice in my head was hoisting a red flag, but I ignored it by thinking about all of the trouble I was facing from all sides and the general lack of support I was receiving.

I take a change of clothes, a cooler with food and drink, my PC, and my briefcase. As I pull onto Interstate 75 North, I feel somehow excited and reserved at the same time. I finally feel as if I'm doing something to help myself. At the very least, no one will be able to bother me or take away another piece of my pride since I'm going dark for a little while. I realize that being on my own for a time, with no one to bother me, is appealing.

I pull into the state park at about 4:30 p.m. I'm in luck because the ranger's office is closed but there is an envelope with "Mr. Bobo" on it taped to the door. A note inside indicates the key to Unit A-8 is under the floor mat. I'm also instructed to leave $70 in the envelope and slide it through the mail slot on the door. I leave the money and proceed to the A-frame cabin.

The unit is very clean and nice. It sleeps six, and I think briefly that my wife would have liked it here. I feel a brief flash of shame because Linda wouldn't have approved of the reason I'm here, which is basically to come up with a war plan. But I tell myself that I tried to play it nice, and everyone seemed to be against me. I then push further thoughts of Linda and all of my doubts out of my head. I've got an important plan to formalize.

After eating a lunchmeat sandwich and potato chips for dinner, I take a legal pad and pen out of my briefcase. I turn off my cell phone, although no one has called me for a while, and I only have one bar of reception showing on the cell screen. This confirms that I'm really in the boonies. As I try to find a way to make everything right, I'm drawing blanks.

I haven't written anything down yet, and I've come up with nothing after rehashing everything bad that's happened to me over the last four days.

I finally ask myself, "What would make this whole thing go away?" The answer seems easy. Gayle Wade could retract everything she has claimed. I see the odds of this happening as slight because she has no reputation to be worried about losing. She's an ex-con for goodness sakes. Then something comes to me. What if I go to see her, unannounced, and take a recorder with me? Knowing she has no reason to cooperate before receiving some type of financial offer from DPG I have to come up with a way to make her admit the truth.

"Kevin," I say to myself out loud, "if she thinks you're put out enough to shoot her, she'll cooperate." Although this theory has holes in it and puts me outside of the boundaries of the law, it seems to hold water in my current state of mind. I tell myself I've been wronged, and she's the kind of person who will likely need the threat of lethal force to back off of her lies. I think, with gratification and confidence, that I'll get her to admit everything, including that she initiated the only contact between us—an unwanted kiss on my face.

I start to write down my plan in some detail, promising myself I'll destroy this document once my mission is complete. I write the following on a yellow-lined page:

1. Gas up my second car, an old Mercedes, for the three-hour trip to Helena.
2. Alter the license plate number with a Sharpie, white paper, and clear packing tape. The risk of the car being

identified in Alabama is more problematical than being pulled over on the highway.

3. Fill two five-gallon gas cans so there is no need to stop in order to refuel the car before returning home.
4. Clean and load the .22 Beretta. Place seven hollow-point shells in the clip. Engage the safety.
5. Drive to the south side of Atlanta, find a Goodwill store, and pay cash for a black stocking cap, black shirt, and black pants.
6. Go to a retail sporting goods store and pay cash for some eye black to put on my face.
7. Buy a handheld recorder and AAA batteries for it.
8. Sign on to the Internet and find 2–3 small no-frills hotels within a few miles of Wade's house. Call ahead of time to make sure they accept cash. No need to make a reservation since Sunday night should be a time of low occupancy.
9. Locate a good place to dump the gun, if need be, on the way back home.
10. Leave home between 5:00 and 6:00 p.m. and be certain no acquaintances see you leave. If someone does notice you, go home, and consider postponing the trip for twenty-four hours.
11. Wear old tennis shoes used for cutting grass since they'll likely be disposed of and they're worn smooth on the bottoms, assuring they won't leave detailed footprint impressions.
12. Pack a fresh change of clothes complete with underwear, socks, tennis shoes, and toiletries.

13. Make another withdrawal from the ATM in order to have $500 in cash with the clean clothes for any unexpected turn of events.

14. Place the cell phone charger in the glove box of the Mercedes.

15. Try to be flexible and expect that something might go wrong. If a minor complication occurs, deal with it on the run in the most effective manner possible. If things fall apart, call a halt to everything and return home.

I finish the list and check my watch. It's already after 11:00 p.m. I ready myself for bed and decide I need to leave by nine in the morning to have enough time to make all of the necessary preparations and execute the plan tomorrow night. I drift off to sleep and conclude that this direct approach is all I can do besides just wait and let other people and events shape my future. I think that doing something, even if it's somewhat desperate, to fix things is my best course at this point.

The last thing I think about before succumbing to the sandman is that I have to decide what I'll do if Ms. Wade doesn't cooperate in spite of my .22 caliber persuader. I also have to be concerned with the boyfriend, Bob Ireland. He could be a problem if he's in the house when I arrive.

CHAPTER 18

SUNDAY: ONE DAY EARLIER

My travel alarm clock goes off at 8:00 a.m. I'm feeling pretty rested and get out of bed. Now my plan completed late last night doesn't seem to be as solid to me in the light of day. Beginning to have doubts, I take a shower and brush my teeth. I take a few minutes to sit down and decide, once and for all, if I'm going to go through with this paramilitary interrogation.

It has a lot of pros and cons, and the cons include many ways in which I can ruin my life with legal issues that could lead to incarceration. Vague feelings of guilt sneak into my head as I again recall my wife and her values. I see no way she would have considered what I'm planning to be reasonable or remotely right despite what's been done to me.

As I begin to think that just maybe I should back out of this risky option I've thought up, my cell rings. I notice that I now have three bars of reception power. I hit the button on the screen and answer, "Hello."

The caller replies, "Good morning, Kevin. This is Buster Todd. We haven't talked in a few days, and I was hoping I could reach you this morning. Do you have a minute?"

Do I really have a choice? I think, before responding, "Sure, go ahead."

Todd clears his throat and continues, "Everyone at DPG is pulling for you. Your company-provided representative, Counselor Patterson, tells me there's a chance the police have doubts about Ms. Wade's story. Unfortunately, there's no way to gauge the likelihood of this thing going in your favor any time soon. We held a meeting yesterday with the chief counsel for DPG, the vice president of the claim shop in Houston, the public relations area, and the senior vice president of human resources.

"It was a tough call, but the consensus reached in the meeting was that you should be discharged for cause with the option to seek reinstatement to your position when you're cleared in this matter. I want you to know that we discussed all possible positions, including the chance that you might file a wrongful termination suit against Disability Protection Group. But our legal people feel we're on solid ground, and it makes sense, from a publicity standpoint, to cut ties until you're exonerated.

"I'm sorry to deliver this message on a weekend, but a statement should be released from the main office in Houston tomorrow announcing your termination. It was agreed to pay you a six-month separation package with your insurance benefits intact over the same period of time. Your signature on a termination document is, of course, necessary to initiate your payments over the term of the agreement. The paperwork also requires that you not discuss the terms of this settlement with anyone, have no contact with any of our employees or customers, and agree to not bring suit against DPG. An overnight packet detailing all of this will arrive at your home tomorrow. Do you have any questions at this time?"

"Yes," I say. "Does the company plan to continue to foot the bill for my representation by Patterson? Also, what if it takes me longer than six months to clear my name?"

"Those are good questions. I'll need to get back to you on them. Anything else you can think of now?" Todd asks.

I am getting pretty mad but hold my tongue and state, "No, not until I read the paperwork. I would say thanks for calling me, but I have to tell you I feel like I've had my legs cut out from under me. I need to get off of this call before I say something I regret."

Todd offers a shallow apology, again promising I'll receive the package tomorrow and that I can call with any questions or further concerns. He breaks the connection, and I'm stunned, to say the least. I momentarily wonder about a couple of oddball things. *When will I lose my cell phone and PC?* I quickly realize these are minor concerns. Then a powerful rush rages through my skull, and I say out loud, "Look out, Gayle Wade. I'm definitely coming to see you."

9:00 A.M.

I pack up and head back to my home in Alpharetta. It's early afternoon when I arrive, and thankfully, there are no further messages painted on the house, nor are there any other signs of uninvited visitors. I enter the kitchen through the door from the garage and pull out the list I made last night. I put it on the table and review it. I feel energized with a definite set of tasks in front of me. I decide to continue to leave the home phone line disconnected from the wall jack.

The first thing I do is drive my Mercedes to a gas station and fill it up. I also fill two five-gallon gas cans from my garage. They have screw-down lids and pouring spouts. I wear an old ball hat and sunglasses in case there are surveillance cameras. You can't be too careful, I tell myself. I, of course, pay cash for this purchase and return home.

Next, I search online for some Goodwill stores in south Atlanta. I find two and call them. Both are open until 5:00 p.m. Switching back to my other car, I drive to one via my GPS and find what I want. The stocking hat is a little scratchy but sufficient. The black pants and long-sleeved black shirt are both made from a cotton blend and are slightly too big, but they will do. I also buy a cheap pair of black socks. Again, I pay cash for my purchase and depart.

I find an Academy Sports outlet right off of I-85 North and pull into the parking lot. I ask the clerk if they carry eye black, and she directs me to a display adjacent to the cash register. I pay $4.99, again in cash, and return to the car. I go into an electronics store and buy a digital recorder. It costs me $80. I want to have some more money on hand, and I decide to use an ATM owned by another bank, although I doubt if this makes any difference in tracking my cash withdrawals. I authorize a user's fee of $3 and take out $400 to add to the money I have left. I think to myself that this is the only transaction in which I'm leaving an electronic trail, but getting money from a checking account is a common and widespread practice.

I've completed my outside purchases, and everything else I need is at home. I drive into my garage and hit the button to close the door behind me. I check my watch and note it's almost four thirty. *I have plenty of time*, I think to myself happily. I next retrieve my Beretta pistol and clean it. I then fill one of my two empty clips with seven hollow-point shells and insert it in the handle. There might be room for one or two more shells, but I don't think I'll need them. I put the safety in the On position.

Next, I put two AAA batteries in my new recording device. It's similar to the one I used for work, and I'm confident it's reliable. I hope I get to use one of these for work purposes again at some point. I then go into the garage and use a Sharpie to change the numbers on the Mercedes's plate. I tape small pieces of white paper marked such that three existing numbers look different. When I finish, two 6s look like 8s and a 7 looks like a 9. The clear mailing tape holds well, and for kicks and grins, I place a piece of the clear tape over the entire plate giving its surface a more uniform look.

Again, I think it's more important that the correct license plate number not be spotted in Alabama while the car is parked. I'll hope that my luck will hold, and I'm not pulled over by John Q. Law. I'll need to stay at or below the speed limit and avoid anything that could be interpreted as erratic driving.

I pull my PC out one more time and search for a good spot to dump my gun if the need arises. It needs to be on I-20 East between Birmingham and Alabama. I find what appears to be the perfect spot—the Cahaba River. The river flows under the interstate between exits 137 and 138. If circumstances dictate, I can pull off to the side on or near the bridge spanning the river and toss the gun. I think to myself that I will again need to be lucky that no police cars see my car pulled over and decide to check on me. This is another piece of my plan that can't be made risk-free.

I go upstairs and get my leather travel bag. I put the clothes I bought in it along with the eye black, the stocking cap, toiletries, and the Beretta. I add my old scruffy tennis shoes that I use for yard work. This will be their last chore. I also put most of my cash on hand in the bag. I think I'm done and check my list. I notice one more thing, and I run up to the bedroom and grab the cell phone charger that plugs into a cigarette lighter. I put it in the glove box, and that's it. I'm ready.

I lie down and try to nap for a little while, but I'm too wired to fall asleep. After thirty minutes, I give up and go downstairs. I'm not hungry but manage to eat a baloney sandwich since I'm not sure when I'll get around to eating again. I close my eyes and think about all of the heartache Gayle Wade has caused me. If I can get her to confess her lies on tape, I'll finally have something in my possession to fight back with. I only hope it'll be enough.

CHAPTER 19

SUNDAY

6:15 P.M.

I 'm on my way via I-20 West, and the old Mercedes is purring smoothly. I have the feel of being on an assignment similar to the appointments I scheduled for work. I think about the fact I have never travelled with a gun before, which is a little unnerving. But I then recite to myself all of the issues I've endured over the last few days including my reputation; my standing in the community; the support of my church; my income; my job; my sense of well-being; and, maybe most importantly, control of my life.

Reminding myself to remain calm, I try to think of possible alternatives I can pursue instead of my current course. The Disability Protection Group attorney is worried about the company, not me. Mr. Patterson, my Birmingham attorney, seems about as useful as fool's gold; he's not doing anything as far as I can tell. The Birmingham police have referred to me as a person of interest. I don't see them being concerned about my problems. My church has pretty much categorized me as persona non grata and, for all practical purposes, expelled me.

I tell myself that my current plan to secure some type of confession from Gayle Wade appears to be the only course I can pursue. Can it go wrong? It sure can, I admit to myself. However, if I play my cards right, I think I can survive almost any outcome in dealing with her. If the worst happens, and she refuses to admit her lies, I can leave and quickly return home after getting rid of my clothes and, if need be, dump the gun. Sure, she can notify the authorities of my visit, but if I can make it home unscathed, it'll be her word against mine, and I'm no worse off than I am now. At least I hope not.

I tell myself I have a reasonable expectation that if I make this trip and return home without anyone being the wiser, I'll be no worse off regardless of the outcome. *Success is certainly not guaranteed*, I admit to myself, *but at least I'm doing something to try to improve my lot, and that goal doesn't seem to be on anyone else's agenda.*

It's about 9:45 p.m. (CST) when I pull into the isolated Tide Terrace, named after this state's beloved University of Alabama football, I presume. There are only three cars in the weed-strewn parking lot, two of them near a front entrance flanked with a neon sign that reads "Office." I remark to myself that this place looks rundown, seedy, and on its last leg. In other words, it's perfect!

I stroll nonchalantly into the office and find an overweight clerk sleeping behind a glass window with a drawer mechanism for transactions that keeps the customers of this "fine" establishment completely separated from the crack staff (or is it the staff on crack?). I knock on the window and wake him. I ask him for a room, and he wants to know for how many people. I tell him only me, and he gives me a look as if he doesn't believe me.

He then asks me for a credit card and my ID to pay the nightly rate of $40. I tell him I'm paying cash, and I left my ID in the car. He smiles and asks my name, to which I reply, "Josh Johnson." He writes this down on something in front of him, and I hand him a fifty. He says he's not sure if he has the right change and can find nothing but a five—and only one five at that—in the drawer. I know I'm being conned but tell him it's all right and that I'll accept $5 in change. He hands me a room key to unit no. 16 and the $5, and I thank him. Smiling, I head back to my car and park it near no. 16. I unlock the door and begin making my preparations.

10:00 P.M.

I decide to make a reconnaissance drive-by to view Ms. Wade's house to be sure she's home. If she seems to be gone, I can repeat my plan tomorrow night with the exception of selecting a different no-star hotel. Using my GPS, I find the home at the end of the dead-end street. There are no cars present other than the old out-of-service Camaro I saw during the field visit a couple of weeks ago. It seems impossible when I think of all that has transpired since that time, all of it bad.

There are lights on in the small house, and I see someone moving about. I drive just past it and slowly turn around at the road's circular end. As I make a second pass by the place, I switch off my lights. I sit at the end of her driveway for a couple of minutes and, finally, there! I can see Ms. Wade walking in front of the living room window into an adjoining room. She's carrying some dishes and is moving around in a smooth, brisk gait. My blood boils as I see her appearing quite healthy. My stomach clenches as I think of all the grief her lies have caused me over the last few days. I roll slowly up the road toward the cross-street before accelerating and turning on my car lights. I head back to the Tide Terrace, feeling excited but also a little apprehensive.

Five minutes later, I turn back into the hotel parking lot. There are now only two cars besides mine. It's not quite 10:30 p.m., and I sit in my car for a minute to think. What I'm about to do is daring and, to be honest, unlawful—probably in more ways than one. I tell myself that I can just pack it in and drive home right now, and no one will be the wiser. But if I do this, I'm back in a situation where my life is being completely controlled by the actions of other people. This hasn't worked too well so far.

Well, I think, *I'm here. I have what I need, and maybe I can talk some sense into this damn woman.* I lock up my car and go into the room. I take off my clothes and shoes and lay them on the dresser. I put a clean pair of underwear and socks with them. I make sure the hotel has a clean towel, wash cloth, and bar of soap in the bathroom. There's even a small plastic bottle of shampoo which I move from the sink to the shower stall.

Now I put on the black shirt and black pants. I roll up the legs of the longish pant legs a little. I put the black stocking hat on and sit down to put on a pair of dark socks and the old worn-out tennis shoes. I stand in front of the mirror and apply the eye black to my forehead, nose, and cheeks. I look a little scary and hope this works to my advantage.

I can't take any ID with me, so I put my wallet under my clothes on the dresser. I think I'm ready and realize I nearly forgot the Beretta. I take the gun out of my duffel bag and make sure the safety is still engaged. Then I put it in my left pocket as I'm left-handed. I have the door set to lock when I close it. I place the room key in my left back pocket and button it shut. I put my handheld recorder in my right back pocket.

I think of leaving my cell phone in the room but reconsider in case I might need it for who knows what reason. I turn off the ringer and put it in my right front pocket. I'm ready. I sit down on the edge of the bed and watch the clock to make sure it's after 11:00 p.m. when I leave. I'm nervous, and as I wait, I notice a twitch in my right calf. At 11:05 p.m., I leave the room for what may be the most important forty-five minutes of my life. I'm soon to find out that I'll be gone for a little while longer than that.

CHAPTER 20

SUNDAY—THE UNOFFICIAL WADE FIELD VISIT

11:20 P.M.

My first order of business is to find a good place to leave the car. I don't want anyone to see it at Wade's house. I find a good spot just off the road that her street runs into. It doesn't appear to be part of anyone's yard, and I park the Mercedes behind a copse of trees about fifteen feet from the road. *This is perfect*, I think. I pray this is an omen that things will go well tonight as I place the car keys next to the room key in my back pocket.

I've already engaged the button on the dash to kill the interior lights so it remains dark when I open the door. I get out of the car and feel almost electrically charged with excitement and anticipation. My senses seem to be honed to a razor's edge as I hear a car approaching a good thirty seconds before it passes by on the other side of the trees. I close my eyes to more quickly acclimate them to the darkness. A crescent moon provides reasonable light as I make my way toward the road.

I stay about ten feet off the side of the road as I approach Wade's cul-de-sac on foot. Fortunately, no cars go by, so I'm not forced to worry about whether or not I'm visible to any passing motorists. I turn down her street but see I'm going to be more exposed because the woods are very thick on both sides of the street. I decide that if a car turns down the street, I may have to freeze, remain motionless, and hope I'm not seen. Again, good fortune comes my way. No cars turn down the street.

The Wade place is about two hundred feet down the cul-de-sac, almost at the very end. I pass two other houses on the road, one on each side. No lights are on in either place, more good fortune. As I approach her house, I see the lights are still on. *Good,* I think. *I'll be able to pinpoint her location and not have to enter blind.* I get down on my hands and knees and creep forward as soon as I leave the road. I reach the old Camaro and sit for a second, leaning against the car door away from the house. I take a deep breath and slowly make my way to the picture window in a crouch.

Again, I feel tingly and am aware of the sounds around me. I hear bugs buzzing and cars in the distance. I stand about ten feet from the big window, so I'm, hopefully, not visible to anyone inside. I wait for what seems like forever and begin to wonder if she has gone to bed and left the lights on. I think to myself this may not be a bad idea in such an isolated location. But then, she walks into the living room.

I can see her in great detail. She's wearing a white tee shirt and blue jeans. I can't see her feet, but I would guess she's barefoot. Her hair is neatly combed back and looks better than it did when I interviewed her. Then I look closer and see her face is wet, and she appears to be drying tears from her eyes. And suddenly, she buries her face in her hands and sobs so loudly it's like I'm right next to her. I can't believe what I'm seeing. I thought of her as something close to a monster—a lying, fraudulent, cheating ex-convict. That is not the image of the person in front of me right now. She appears to be forlorn, almost as if mourning someone's death. A thought rushes into my head, and although it's unwanted, it forces its way in: She's a person to pitied, not hated.

This sudden contradiction of feelings throws me into a state of uncertainty. My knees become weak, and I kneel down for a few seconds. And to my surprise, despite all that this woman has done to me, I begin to feel sorry for her. I think of my deceased wife, Linda, and I know for sure that she would want me to forgive this woman, not get even with her. I think she'd even be inclined to forgive the pastor who effectively excommunicated me from my church.

I remain on one knee for a short time to regain my composure. Despite all that I've endured over the past couple of weeks, I realize I can't stoop to the level of Gayle Wade in trying to reclaim my life. If I do, I'm no better than she is. I can't believe I have a loaded gun in my pocket. What was I thinking? I'm flooded with a sense of relief and gratitude that I didn't carry through with my plan. I glance up and see Ms. Wade sitting on a dilapidated couch with her head in her hands, obviously still crying.

I surprise myself as I have an urge to go inside and comfort her but acknowledge that this would be a foolish thing to do. I'm preparing to quietly make an exit when something unexpected takes place. A car pulls in the driveway, momentarily flashing its headlights in my direction. I hit the ground and lie flat. My heart rate accelerates to the point I fear it can be heard by whoever just pulled up. To my astonishment, I see the boyfriend, Bob Ireland, step out of the car and walk toward the house. He's wearing a hoodie.

I tell myself it's time to get out of here, but I can't tear my eyes away from the window, only a few feet away. Ireland storms into the house, pushing the front door so hard that it rams into the adjacent wall. He yanks the hoodie off of his head and screams, "What's wrong with you, Gayle? What was that garbage you were spouting on the phone earlier?"

Ms. Wade looked at him, her eyes swollen and red, and responds, "It's time to stop this nonsense, Bob. This thing's not going to work other than to get us both in a lot of trouble."

At this moment, I make one of those decisions that you think back on later and know you wouldn't do it one time out of a hundred normally. But besides some concern for Gayle at the hands of this seemingly explosive man, I come to the conclusion that I'm still in a huge mess, even though I've recaptured some measure of good judgment. From what little I just heard pass between these two flawed people, I think I might be interested in getting the rest of this conversation on tape. Therefore, I crawl up to the window, the bottom of which is partially open, with a screen in place to admit a breeze. I take the tape recorder out of my right-side back pocket, click it to the Record position and set it on the ledge. I move back a few steps so I'm not too visible and watch. Then things begin to get interesting.

Ireland yells, "You crazy damn broad! We have to see this through. Your shyster lawyer said the insurance company will probably be willing to settle out of court, but we have to be patient. It hasn't been that long. Why would you want to give up now?"

Wade answers in a low, almost calm voice, "Bob, you know I've been in trouble before. The cops haven't been back in touch with us since the complaint was filed. I've done time and have a lot on my record. They probably don't believe me anyway."

Ireland retorts, "What good does it do us to give up now? My ass is on the line here, you know. I backed up your story that the interviewer guy messed with you in your bed. If we get some money to split with the lawyer, I don't care what the cops end up doing."

I think to myself that I may have enough recorded right now to clear my name. I decide to hang in a little longer and see what happens. Wade stands up, raises her arms slightly upward, and says, "I thought we were a couple, Bob. That doesn't have to change if we get out of this without facing charges. I thought you loved me." Her facial expression tells me she really doesn't believe this to be true but wants it to be.

Ireland quickly dispels any hopes she may have been holding on to when he shouts, "How can I love a psycho that goes back on her word? Tell me, how?"

A look of loss blankets Wade's face, and she says in a meek voice, "I've had enough. I'm going to see the police in the morning, with or without the lawyer. I'm telling them the truth and that the disability rep didn't do anything to me. I'm going to hope they go easy on me, although they probably shouldn't."

Ireland seemed frozen solid and gives her a vicious stare for what seemed like an eternity. Then he takes a gun out of his pocket, and I nearly lose control of my bowels. He points it at her, and she actually smiles and says, "Go ahead. You'd be doing me a favor."

I find myself inching closer to the window and tell myself he won't shoot; he's only trying to scare her. Then the gun goes off, and it sounds like a bomb. I see Wade go down with a crimson stain spreading outward from her abdomen. I can't believe my eyes and scream at the top of my lungs, "Noooo!"

This is a big mistake. Ireland immediately looks out the window, spots me, and says in a monotone and eerily calm voice, "You…here? Good." To my horror, he almost seems to be salivating as he stares.

Somehow, I have the presence of mind to grab the recorder from the window ledge and stuff it in my pocket. I spin and sprint for the woods at the end of the cul-de-sac. Just before entering the trees, I hear a second shot. I don't know if the madman is shooting at me or not, but I'm not going to hang around to find out. As I break into the foliage on a dead run, I hear sounds of Ireland pursuing me. Then he yells at me, "You're dead, you're dead!" Feeling a wave of fear mixed with anger, I think in silent reply, *Maybe so, but I'll make it as hard as possible for you.*

CHAPTER 21

MONDAY: PRESENT DAY

2:30 A.M.

I'm in a fog. I know something's terribly wrong, but I can't figure out what it is. Slowly, I start to remember things, but not in their logical order. I know I'm exhausted and vaguely recall being cut, bruised, and beaten by limbs, bushes, thorns, and rocks. My whole body feels like it's been through a meat grinder. My eyes are out of focus when I try to look around, so I close them. I can feel wet socks on my feet but no shoes.

Then, with a start, I remember Gayle Wade being shot. I wonder if somehow I shot her but almost immediately realize it was Bob Ireland. At this time, memories begin flooding back into my head until I think it'll explode—the secret trip to Alabama, the Beretta and change of clothes, the Tide Terrace and its dirty carpet, the word *pervart* painted on my garage door, losing my job, the argument between Ireland and

Gayle before the shooting, and being chased for what seemed like forever through the woods.

I open my eyes again slowly, and as they struggle to focus, I determine I'm lying on a hard surface. As my vision slowly clears, I see I'm inside a house. My hands are lying by my sides, and as I move my left one a little, it bumps into something hard. I look downward and see it's my gun. I touch the barrel, and it's slightly warm. I sit up quickly and fight back a wave of nausea. I see another gun close to my right hand, and this one is bigger than mine.

All of a sudden, I think that Ireland might be nearby, and I jump up. I nearly faint as I find myself looking at the body of Gayle Wade in a pool of blood. "Oh my God!" I yell out and stumble backward. Loudly, I say, "Is anyone here?" And there is no response. I then recall passing out as Ireland was approaching me with his gun near the house that was under construction. Now, I think I understand. He's trying to frame me for the murder of Gayle. He probably thought I'd be unconscious when the police arrive.

I force myself to look more closely at the body and see three places where it looks like she's been shot. I remember hearing two shots when I ran from her house and two more being fired over my head in the woods. Where did her third wound come from? Wait a minute! I check the clip on my Beretta and count the shells. There are only six, and I distinctly remember loading seven. I'm sure I never fired the gun or even nudged off the safety.

Now I'm thinking the other gun is probably the one Ireland used. It's a good bet my fingerprints are on both guns; they were probably pressed into my hands while I was out. I hear police sirens in the distance. I have to assume they're on the way here. I quickly make a decision not to be here when the cops arrive. I put a gun in each pocket. I hope neither one fires, but I don't think they will.

I go into the kitchen and grab a dish towel. I clean the hardwood floor where I was lying without touching the blood. I look around quickly and don't see anything else I think ties me to the scene. I use the towel to clean the door knob and also use it on the outside doorknob. It's dark and quiet outside, but the sirens appear to be getting closer. I have no idea what time it is. I check my watch and see it's just after 2:30 a.m. I stuff the dish towel inside my trousers and begin walking down the dead-end street to the intersection where my car is hidden. I hope and pray there is nothing in the house indicating I was there.

At this moment, a police car turns down the street. It has no lights on, but now the driver turns on the headlights, the bar lights, the red lights, and the siren. I freeze for a second and then dive into the ditch. With my face down, I close my eyes and pray I wasn't seen. The car screeches past me and brakes to a stop at the Wade house. I crawl toward the end of the street and then skirt through some trees toward where I remember leaving my car.

I panic when I don't find it and sit on the ground, hyperventilating. I can probably work my way back to the hotel, but how will I get home? I get up and begin walking toward the road, enter a clearing and—all right!—there sits the Mercedes. For a second, I convince myself I've surely managed to lose the key during the wild chase, but they're in my back pocket along with the room key. The engine purrs to life, and I sit there for a short time in case other police cars or emergency vehicles show up. I definitely don't want to be spotted.

After a few minutes, I pull slowly onto the road with my lights out and drive away from the dead-end street. When I've gone a fourth of a mile, I turn the headlights on and continue at the posted speed limit of 30 mph. I reach the Tide Terrace at 2:40 a.m. I pull into the parking lot, and there is only one other car, right next to the office. It probably belongs to Mr. Short Change.

I know it's early in the game, but I allow myself the luxury of thinking I just might get out of this. I remind myself not to think ahead because I still have a long, risky way to go. I reach into my back pocket and take out the room key. I enter the room, and everything is as I left it. I look in the mirror and am shocked. I'm a total mess. My shirt is ripped, and my face has bloody cuts and scratches. My pants are wet and muddy, and my black socks are wet and torn. I have stickers and thorns on my arms, legs, clothes, and in my hair.

I take the guns—one in each front pocket—out and put them in the top drawer of the chest, closing it. I remove the trash liner from the waste can and start taking off my clothes. I put all of my clothing, including my underwear and socks, in the plastic liner. I tie a knot in it at the top. I then reinspect myself in the mirror and begin picking burrs, stickers, and thorns off of me. I have to work several out of my shortly cropped hair and notice some small cuts on the top of my head.

I take my clean clothes out of my duffel bag and lay them on the bed. I have a tee shirt, shorts, underwear, socks, belt, and tennis shoes. I also take out my wallet, with the extra cash, and lay it next to my clothes. I grab the deodorant, comb, and hair gel and take them into the bathroom. I smile to myself because I guess I was worried about my hair looking okay. What a crazy thing to have been thinking about. I go back into the room to be sure the door is locked. I stand quietly for a moment and hear nothing from the outside or on either side of the room.

I go back to the bathroom and turn on the shower. The water stream is surprisingly strong, and it quickly becomes hot. I step under the water and jump backward as my numerous cuts sting like the devil. I ease back in and let the clean water do its trick. Soon, I feel better and begin soaping up, although this stings too. After I rinse the soap off, I feel better. I work some hotel shampoo into my hair and start thinking to myself, *What am I forgetting?* Then it occurs to me in a flash of realization. *Where is my recorder?*

I literally fly out of the shower and land with a damp thud. I rip into the trash liner and confirm the recorder isn't in any of my pants pockets. I start shaking all over as I dry off with the cheap, thin hotel towel.

I run the events of the evening through my mind, and I remember the last place I saw the recorder was on the window ledge of Wade's house below the partially opened window. *No, wait!* I think to myself. *I grabbed it and stuffed it into my right pocket before I ran away from Ireland, I'm sure. That's the last time I saw it, without a doubt.* I tell myself that I took such a wild run, including falling into a pond, while being chased it could be lying anywhere in the woods or the water. Then a chilling thought came to me and I shake even more violently. *What if Ireland took it out of my pocket when he moved me to the murder scene?*

In this split second, I realize that I have come to the definitive conclusion that the reason I ended up at the murder scene was because Ireland put me there. I can't remember anything from the time I blacked out until I came to next to poor Ms. Wade, but there doesn't seem to be any other logical possibility. He must have wanted to frame me for the murder. I'm also pretty certain the guns have my fingerprints on them, and who knows? Ireland may have fired from one or both guns with my hand on the grips and triggers when I was still unconscious. The world seems to be closing in on me with this realization and tears begin to flood my eyes as I stumble back into the shower.

The water has started to get cold by the time I finally accept the stark reality that I don't know where the recorder is. I need to assume the worst—that Ireland took it. I get out of the shower a second time and towel myself dry. I begin dressing and check my watch; it's just after 3:00 a.m. or 4:00 a.m. in Alpharetta. I use my deodorant before I finish dressing. I then rub some gel in my hair and use my fingers to give it a halfway decent look. Man, I must be a little conceited or something. I notice my fingers are sore when I work the gel through my hair. I put the deodorant and gel in the duffel and take the trash liner from the waste can in the bathroom. My hands are shaking as I put the guns in this liner and tie it at the top. *These babies are going to be dumped*, I think to myself.

I grab the bag with my ripped, soiled clothes in it and go outside. I find a large dumpster at the end of the parking lot and open the lid. I take a somewhat clean-looking newspaper from the inside and move some of the putrid trash aside. I put the bag with my clothes on the bottom of the container and move other trash back over it. As I walk back to my room, I feel pretty comfortable no one will find this stuff or put two and two together if they do.

Now, it's time to check out of the Terrace. From watching crime shows on TV, I decide to take a towel and wipe down all of the surfaces in the room I may have touched. I also wipe the room key and its plastic attachment with the room number on it. I leave it on the TV. I lay the duffel and the plastic bag with the guns in it just outside the door. I wipe the doorknob on both sides and then throw the towel back inside before shutting the self-locking door. I'm checked out.

I place my duffel in my trunk and the plastic bag with the guns beside me in the other bucket seat. My hands shake slightly as I realize this part of my trip is risky. It's early in the morning, a blessing and a curse. There are fewer cars on the roads, but that makes it easier to be seen. The engine fires up, I turn on my GPS, and pull out onto the road. Fortunately, the GPS doesn't want me to head back toward the Wade house.

I stay alert to the traffic signs and don't exceed the posted speed limits. I think briefly of my uncle who worked for the railroad. He would typically drive home from Louisville to rural Indiana in the wee hours of the morning. He was stopped by Indiana state troopers twice for going too slow; they probably thought he had been drinking. I need to avoid being pulled over for speeding, going slow, or anything else. I pray my luck holds.

I take US 31 South to Interstate 65 North. There are almost no cars. I then drive at 65 miles per hour on Interstate 459 North for a few miles prior to entering Interstate 20 East toward Atlanta. So far, so good. I see a state patrol car parked by the side of the road as I enter I-20. My Internet research, if accurate, confirmed the Cahaba River crossing under the interstate is only a few miles east of the point I accessed just now.

When I see the mile marker 137, I begin slowing and looking for a bridge. I see one ahead of me and a sign announcing the Cahaba River. I pull over to the side of the road on the bridge. This is the scariest part of my ride home. I turn off my lights instead of using a blinker. I jump out with the guns and look over the side. I have to walk east about thirty feet till I'm comfortable the river is directly below me. Leaving the guns in the bag, I drop it downward and hear a splash. I trust the weight of the contents will make it sink. I breathe a sigh of relief. The guns are gone!

I walk slowly back to my running car. Oh no! I see a car coming. I hope and pray it's not a cop. The driver doesn't slow down, shows no signs of seeing me, and blows past. Good! I get back in my car and check my rearview mirror. Everything is clear. I pull my light switch to On and enter the highway. In about twenty seconds, I'm driving the speed limit of seventy. I slow to sixty-nine and turn on the cruise control. With a little luck, I'll be home in less than three hours.

I'm alert to my surroundings like I've never been before. I check out the few cars that pass me and the fewer cars that I pass. I try to determine if cars going the other direction are police cars. I don't identify any. I see no marked police cars during the remainder of the trip.

I'm still wired when I arrive at my neighborhood a little after 7:00 a.m. There are no signs of life at the gated but unguarded entrance. I drive slowly toward my street and house. I halfway expect to see a police car in my driveway waiting to question me at best or arrest me at worst. I can think of no way they can place me at the scene unless they have Ireland in custody.

The house looks quiet and empty, which is good. There are no signs of anyone in the area. I'm thankful no one decorated the garage door for me again as I push the opener on my visor. I drive into the garage and close the door behind me. I get out, open my trunk, and take out the duffel bag. I close the trunk and bend down in front of the license plate. With my fingernails, I work loose the clear tape and the altered numbers depicted on white paper. This only takes about thirty seconds, and I crumple up the tape and paper in my hand.

I reach for the door handle to enter the house and I collapse on the garage floor. I regain enough composure to get up on my feet and again start shaking like I'm freezing. I'm dripping wet with sweat when I begin crying from a strange mixture of fear and relief, realizing I'm lucky to be alive.

I enter my kitchen and check my landline for any messages from the police or anyone else. I then remember I disconnected my primary phone from the wall jack. I go into the living room and reconnect the phone. I walk to the kitchen, sit down, and breathe a sigh of relief that I'm a free man for at least a little while longer. I then remember the sight of Gayle Wade lying in a pool of her own blood and cry softly for a few minutes.

Despite what she did to me, she didn't deserve to die like that. I think to myself that it wouldn't be so bad if Ireland drove off of a cliff and eliminated himself. I know there is little chance of that happening.

I head to my bedroom and find myself missing my dogs. I throw my clothes into the dirty clothes basket and put on a clean tee shirt with *Oklahoma State Cowboy Basketball* on it. I think I have pulled off the evening's events pretty well with two unplanned exceptions—the missing recorder and the appearance of Bob Ireland. I fall asleep trying to decide which one is more likely to get me in trouble. I come to the conclusion it's Ireland before I drift off.

CHAPTER 22

MONDAY

I sleep until about 11:00 a.m. and am awakened by the phone ringing. I think fearfully it might be the police, but it's a wrong number. For the first time I can remember, I'm grateful for a mistaken phone call. I get up and eat some cereal and drink a glass of orange juice. I sign on to my PC and check the *Birmingham Sentinel*, but there is no coverage of Wade's demise. I listen to the local news, and likewise, no mention of it is made.

I take a shower and am pleasantly surprised that my abrasions and cuts no longer sting too badly when soap and water touch them. I get out of the shower and towel myself dry. I have one bad cut on my right foot, and I find some anti-bacterial cream and a cloth Band-Aid to dress it. I check my face in the mirror and have only one scratch that is visible on my forehead. A couple of more significant cuts are in my hair are not readily seen.

After dressing, I go to the garage and pull out in my Trailblazer. I drive to the boarding facility in Marietta to pick up my dogs. I show my receipt of payment, and they bring the dogs to the reception area. After letting them settle down a little, I take them to the car and put them in the back where they share space with my golf clubs. As I drive home, I think about my wild weekend and am glad that I managed to return to my senses before confronting Wade. It also would have been even more catastrophic if I'd been in the house when Ireland arrived. I feel worried about the recorder but decide it is likely not an issue. If it's lost in the woods, it may be inoperable or never found by anyone.

If Ireland got his hands on it, he most likely destroyed it as it records his act of murder. I calculate again that there's a reasonable chance he pulled it out of my pocket, assuming he took me back to the house and arranged things in an attempt to implicate me in the murder. I still can't come up with a more plausible scenario that brings me from a chase through the woods, passing out and waking up next to a dead body.

The dogs and I arrive at home in the early afternoon, and they are happy to be there. When I go inside, I have a message on my home phone. I listen and almost lose control of my bowels. It's Detective Skirvin of the Birmingham Police Department. He asks that I return his call. I start shaking and wonder if I'm about to be in big trouble. I tell myself that if this were the case, the local police would probably be picking me up to send me to Birmingham, but I'm not completely sure.

With a shaky hand, I dial the number the detective left on my machine. When I indicate who I'm calling, a receptionist quickly connects me to the Sex Crimes Unit. Detective Skirvin comes on the line and says, "Thanks for calling back, Mr. Harrington. I have some news that may surprise you. Before I tell you about it, I have to ask you a question. Where were you from six last night until six this morning?" I'm shaken to the core. Do they suspect I'm involved? I decide to take a chance and stick with my prepared story, "I was home. I went to a state park in Tennessee to get away on Saturday and got back last evening. I didn't go anywhere elsewhere until about an hour ago when I picked up my dogs."

I immediately think to myself, *Idiot! You boarded them under a false name.* Well, it was too late now. I had spilled those beans. Detective Skirvin then asked, "Can anyone vouch for you being home last evening and overnight?"

I told him, "No, sir. I'm widowed and live by myself."

He said, "Okay. Here's the news I have for you. Gayle Wade was murdered last night. She was shot multiple times by more than one gun. Do you own a gun?"

I quickly think that there is no way he can put me owning a gun, and I respond, "No. Who did it?"

He replied, "We're not sure, but we have our suspicions. You remember the boyfriend, Mr. Ireland? I'm sure you do. He seems to have disappeared. We have a BOLO out on him and hope to pick him up." I think to myself, *Good gravy, do I want him caught or not? He might try to blame me and put me at the scene. Maybe I should come clean now with the detective.*

No, I tell myself. *Sit tight and see what happens.* I can always tell the truth and hope for forgiveness later if it comes to that.

Detective Skirvin then relates, "By the way, I wanted to let you know something else. We never seriously considered that you had tried to assault Ms. Wade. Her background is sketchy, and she was a career criminal who had served time. It was our working theory that she and Ireland were scheming to try and force a financial settlement from your employer." My jaw dropped when I heard this; I probably never had to do anything but sit tight and be exonerated! Man, I wish I had known this earlier.

I blurt out, "Why didn't you tell me this? I lost my job over this thing."

He simply says, "Sorry about that. Hope you get it back."

I then said, forcefully, "Why did you tell the newspaper I was a person of interest?"

He replied, "We wanted Wade and the boyfriend to think their scheme was on track. Plus, by virtue of being accused, you were technically a suspect. We were preparing to question them this week and try to poke holes in their story. I would've given your employer the real lowdown if they had contacted me."

Score another one for the brilliant Attorney Patterson, I thought. I say goodbye and hang up before I lose my cool.

I'm stunned by the detective's admission. I think about calling the company attorney, Todd, but decide not to do so. I'll wait till I get the termination package first and then contact him. Maybe he'll find out I was never an actual suspect and stop the firing process. Or maybe I should sue Disability Protection for wrongful termination. Who knows? Maybe I should find out if I can sue Patterson, the inept Birmingham attorney who was supposed to act in my best interests. That's bull, I think to myself. He was acting in the company's best interests.

I stay inside the house for the rest of the day, and the phone only rings once. It's my mother, and I decide to fill her in on everything except my little secret trip. To my surprise, she has little to say other than she hopes the police publicly clear me and offer me an apology. She adds that she thinks I should get to keep my job, and I should change churches. I tell her that's a good suggestion. We confirm that we love each other and mutually end the call.

In the evening, I call my two children and fill them in on the latest developments regarding Ms. Wade. My daughter says she probably got what she had coming to her and I remain silent. My son says I should consider suing DPG, the Wade estate, and the City of Birmingham for defamation of character or some other charge. *If only he knew exactly what kind of character I am*, I think. I feel good that my kids both support me. I wonder if full disclosure on my part would change that.

I go to bed at 11:30 p.m. after watching the evening news. I switch around to the two other network affiliates a few times but hear nothing about the Wade murder. I go to bed exhausted. I surmise that my weekend activities have finally caught up to me. The last thing I see in my mind's eye before nodding off is the evil grin on Ireland's face as he points his gun and walks toward me. Thankfully, I sleep through the night without dreaming or waking up.

CHAPTER 23

TUESDAY

I wake up at 8:30 a.m. and feel pretty good. I sign on to the *Birmingham Sentinel* website and find a front-page story about the Wade murder. It mentions that the police are looking for Ireland as the dreaded person of interest but to no avail. Thankfully, I'm not mentioned, nor are any details of her prior assertion of sexual assault.

I decide to make myself wait until this afternoon before I consider calling Buster Todd of the DPG legal department. I drive to the gas station and buy some gas for my riding lawn mower. I return home and eat some toast and cereal. I put on some grungy clothes and do some yard work. I trim my hedges, edge the yard, and then mow it with my self-propelled mower and riding mower. It looks neat and clean, just the way I like it.

I also do a critical check of my garage door and am pleasantly surprised. I can't see any indication that the door was recently repainted, and there is no sign of the offending words that were put on it by the neighborhood mental midget and spelling champion. I take a quick shower and put on some clean clothes and check the clock; it's 1:45 p.m. The postman has delivered the mail, and I have nothing from Diasability Protection. I recall that Mr. Todd told me the severance package was being overnight expressed. As I'm about to pick up the phone and call him, it rings.

In what is becoming a routine event, I experience another near-tachycardia event when I lift the receiver off of its base. I say, "Hello," and hear a familiar voice.

"Hi, Kevin. This is Buster Todd. How are you?"

I can't stop myself from replying, "Unemployed, I guess, but otherwise fine."

Todd chuckles, and I think to myself this may be a good sign. Todd continues, "I'm assuming you've heard that the woman who accused you is now deceased. I talked with Mr. Patterson, the attorney consulting with us on your behalf in Birmingham, this morning. He said he spoke with the local police, and they consider the assault charge she tried to file against you to be closed.

"He also told me the police never really considered her complaint to be valid, but for the life of me, I don't know why they weren't clear on this earlier. Mr. Patterson thinks their statements made to the press may have been intended to convince Ms. Wade they were seriously investigating her charges when they were actually looking more closely at her background. Did you know she has a record and was in prison?"

This question angers me a little, and I say, "Yes, Buster, I knew that. My interview notes and the research I Federal Expressed to you clearly showed she had a questionable background."

He ignores my barb and replies, "Well, its Patterson's opinion now that you were never facing any appreciable risk of being charged or even investigated."

I want to tell him I think Patterson is incompetent but don't see how that can help my overall situation, so I just remark, "Good."

Todd then tells me, "And the good news is we aren't sending you a severance package. At this time, I feel comfortable that you are going to be reinstated in your position as a field representative. We have to wait for a sign-off by the CEO, and that could take a few days. I'll let you know when his signature is secured. I also can tell you that your salary will be reinstated, so you don't lose any pay. Of course, you'll be required to sign a hold harmless agreement protecting DPG from any legal action on your part since you were verbally informed you were terminated."

I remain silent for a few seconds before responding, "That sounds really good. I'd love to get back to work." Todd promises to call me in the next few days with an update, and we exchange good-byes. I feel as if a huge weight has been lifted off of me. At least my financial health is about to be resuscitated. I spend the next thirty minutes calling my mother and two kids. I want them to know I'm solvent again.

I make myself a glass of sweet tea and sit on my back deck to think things through a little. I admit to myself that I still have a big potential problem in the person of Bob Ireland. The odds are good, I surmise again, that he considers me a loose end. I try to put myself in his shoes, and when I do, I view myself as a big risk. I still think he tried to frame me, which I'm grateful for because otherwise, I'd probably be dead. He has to be concerned that I might go to the police, and for all he knows, I might have kept his gun. I think he has to view me as a big liability at best and, more likely, a real threat to him. I might have this all wrong, but I conclude that I have to assume he'll come after me, and I'm far from safe. Man, what a dilemma.

After this uplifting brainstorming session, I go back in the house and avoid utilizing my nonexistent cooking skills by heating up a frozen dinner. *Lucky me*, I think. I feed the dogs some dry dog food that looks about as good as what I'm preparing to consume. I turn on the six o'clock news and freeze when the lead story is the Wade murder.

An attractive female newscaster says, "We have a follow-up to a story we reported on to you last week. As you may recall, we told you that a local Alpharetta man, Kevin Harrington, was accused by a Helena, Alabama, woman of sexual assault during a meeting in her home. Now, the Birmingham police are reporting that the woman, Gayle Wade, was killed in her home yesterday during the early morning hours. No arrests have been made, although the victim's boyfriend has apparently disappeared. He is being sought for questioning by police. Harrington of Alpharetta is not thought to be involved, per a police spokesperson. This is a picture of the boyfriend, Bob Ireland. Take a good look at it. If you see him or have any information as to his whereabouts, please call the number on your screen. Now for local news…"

I realize I've been holding my breath and inhale deeply. My first impression is that the report appears to absolve me of the murder but remains silent on the assault charge. Oh well, it could be worse, I think. As least I wasn't tagged as an accused sexual predator or something. I don't bother to see if there are any reports on the two other network stations. My guess is the local newspapers may have something on the murder in their next editions.

About an hour later, my home phone rings. It's a kid's voice, and I don't recognize it. I hope it isn't going to be some kind of crank call. He says, "Is this Mr. Harrington?" I confirm it is, and he continues, "I just wanted to tell you I'm sorry for spray painting words on your garage last week. I feel bad about it." I asked him to tell me his name and he says, "John DeMumbrum."

That name sounds vaguely familiar, and I ask him, "Is your mother named Joan, and is she the neighborhood association president?"

He hesitates and responds, "Yes."

Well, I think, *isn't this interesting.*

"John," I say, "I like apologies in person instead of over the phone. Would you and your mother be willing to come over and tell me in person you're sorry?" I know this is silly, but I like the idea of this kid asking his self-important mother to come over and grovel a little bit.

He asks me to wait a minute and puts down the phone. I smile. He comes back on and says, "She said this call is plenty enough, and she won't come to your house. But I'm willing to do it. I just have to wait a few days so she doesn't find out."

I feel like I've had my cheap little thrill and tell John that it won't be necessary for him to come over. I also tell him I respect him for being willing to deliver an apology in person, even if his mother isn't big enough to come over. I grin when John laughs and says, "She's sort of a witch but doesn't know it. Thanks, man. Let me know if I can do you a favor or something. I think you're pretty cool."

I tell John I like him too and end the call. At least, I tell myself, I've probably improved my chances of any future graffiti sprayed on my house being spelled correctly.

I watch some TV over the rest of the evening but don't pay a lot of attention. I'm anxious to see the papers over the next couple of days and also to hear more about my pending job reinstatement. But in the back of my mind, the Bob Ireland issue keeps popping into my head, and I can't talk to anyone about it. I check my door locks and make sure all of my windows are closed tight and secured before I go to bed.

CHAPTER 24

WEDNESDAY

The Atlanta paper arrives in the morning, and the Alpharetta paper will next publish tomorrow. I scan the pages and find an article about the murder in the section devoted to regional news. It's a short Associated Press article and reads as follows:

ALABAMA WOMAN FOUND SHOT TO DEATH

Gayle Wade of Helena, Alabama, was found dead in her home early Sunday morning, the apparent victim of a homicide. Wade was lying in a pool of blood, and police described the scene as looking like a "bloody battlefield." A spokesperson for the Birmingham, Alabama, Police Department, who were called in by local law enforcement authorities, confirmed the deceased died as a result of three gunshot wounds, two to the body and one to her head. No arrests have been made, but Ms. Wade's boyfriend, Bob Ireland, is being sought for questioning. The victim was forty-two years old and is survived by a sister, Ms. Anne Berg of Tucson, Arizona. Funeral arrangements are pending the release of the body from the coroner's office.

No mention of me, I think to myself. It may be better that way, although I would have considered the mention of me *not* being questioned or sought after a retraction of sorts. Anyway, I'm glad it was written in such a way that Ireland looks like the perpetrator as opposed to me, the formerly accused "predator." I eat breakfast and do some much-needed minor cleaning chores around the house. I decide to call my housekeeper in the next few days and confirm the upcoming biweekly cleaning sessions again.

At 11:00 a.m., the phone rings, and as seems to be my routine now, I start shaking with nervous anticipation. I answer, and a female voice asks, "I have Buster Todd, attorney for Disability Protection Group on the other line. Can you talk to him?" I respond in the affirmative, and she asks me to hold. After what seems like an eternity but is probably about thirty seconds, Todd begins talking, "How are you today, Kevin?" I reply that I'm fine but think to myself I'd better if I were once again employed.

Todd says, "Everything has been wrapped up at the DPG home office in your favor. The powers that be have agreed that your position with the company should be reinstated with retroactive salary privileges. Congratulations!"

I think to myself that he is a bit of a sanctimonious wind bag, but I answer simply, "Thanks."

Todd continues, "Of course, we need your signature on the hold harmless agreement first. It's being Federal Expressed to you today with a prepaid overnight envelope to return the executed document. You'll need to have your signature on the paperwork notarized. Any problems with that?"

I respond, "No."

He adds, "We should be able to wrap this up by the end of the day Friday with the receipt of your returned paperwork, and you can start working again on Monday. We'll contact your immediate supervisor and let him know you're back on board so you can resume scheduling and making field visits. Any questions, Kevin?"

I say I have no questions at this time and thank him for calling me. I hang up, breathe a sigh of relief, and think to myself, *One problem solved.*

CHAPTER 25

THURSDAY

I receive the DPG paperwork just before 10:00 a.m. I only have to sign the two-page document at the end of the second page and do so without reading it. A copy is enclosed with the original, and I can peruse it later. I take the document to my bank, and a young lady watches me sign it so she can notarize it. There's no charge since I'm a "preferred customer." I head directly to a Federal Express full service facility and hand the envelope to a clerk who affirms it will be delivered on or before ten tomorrow morning. I smile as I think about returning to work in four days.

When I pull into my driveway at home, I notice the local paper is in the driveway. I grab it and pull into the garage. In the kitchen, I check it out and find a story on the first page of the second section entitled Community News. There is a story on the Wade murder. It reads exactly as did the Atlanta paper's article did yesterday but with one difference—it included a brief paragraph apparently written by the local newspaper staff. I anxiously read this addition to the story.

> An Alpharetta resident, Kevin Harrington of Disability Protection Group, was recently accused of sexually assaulting the deceased. Contact with the Birmingham Police Department confirmed that these charges are now considered moot and will not be pursued. A department spokesperson also acknowledged that the charges are now thought to have not been meritorious—a determination she said was actually made before Ms. Wade was killed.

"Hooray," I say to myself. This is an exoneration if ever I have seen one. Of course, some people will think I'm guilty and just got off on a technicality, but that's unavoidable. It would have been nice if this admission by the police had been made before Ireland killed Wade, but beggars can't be choosers, and I'll take this state of affairs compared to what things were like last week.

Later in the day, my home phone rings, and I try to settle my nerves before picking it up. It's Dr. Day, the pastor of my church. *This should be good*, I think silently. He speaks to me in a jittery voice, "I'm thrilled that your troubles seem to have gone away. It's an answer to prayer. I hope you don't harbor any resentment to me or the church."

Well, not to the church, I say to myself before replying, "No, I understand your situation. I was accused of a horrible thing, and being innocent didn't seem to keep my reputation from being ruined. I'm certainly glad my life seems to be coming back together now."

Dr. Day then indicates, "You're still a beloved member of our congregation. Please disregard my last call to you and chalk it up to a wrong decision being made. I couldn't be more sorry for these actions."

I can't resist rubbing his nose in it a little and reply, "Do I need to take a lie detector test or anything?" I immediately feel guilty and regret the comment, so I add, "Hey, I didn't mean that. I was just hurt that no one backed me up in my time of need. I felt abandoned."

"And for that," Dr. Day says, "I'll always feel ashamed. I hope you can forgive me."

Thinking that I'm far from perfect or even good, I answer, "Let's forget it ever happened. I have a lot of friends in the church, and I probably would've heard from some of them if I hadn't disconnected my phone."

Dr. Day sounds relieved as he remarks, "You do have friends, and I can tell you without a doubt you are loved. I hope you believe me when I tell you I'm praying that I never fail you as your pastor again." I let him know that I'm not harboring any resentment, even though I really am. He also tells me I am needed in the youth Sunday school, and he hopes I'll resume teaching the tenth grade boys' class. I reply that I'm planning to attend the service this Sunday as well as teach the boys the planned curriculum for this week. Pastor Day assures me he'll inform the youth minister of my return. We exchange some more pleasantries before ending the call.

I could look into switching churches, but I have a lot of connections at the one I've attended for the past several years, and I enjoy working with the kids. I decide to swallow my pride and give things a try. I think to myself that everything on the home front and jobwise has turned around 180 degrees in the space of a few days. I feel guilty that it required the forfeiture of a woman's life to accomplish it.

At this moment, my doorbell rings, and lo and behold, it's my would-be neighborhood girlfriend with a paper plate stacked with goodies. Apparently, she's heard the news that I'm off the hook. I greet her with a smile and a hi. She says nothing about the poop escapade and grins at me demurely. I take the plate, thank her, and quickly shut the door before she can say anything. I have no interest in seeing her, but she is a good cook. I guess I have no shame. However, one thing I think I do have is a big loose end named Ireland. I choke a little when swallowing the first of my fresh chocolate chip cookies.

CHAPTER 26

THREE MONTHS LATER

Things have settled back into a normal routine for me. My job is going well, and I am back on my usual schedule of flying a couple of times a week and driving to a closer interview once a week. There was no upheaval when I remained in the church, and in fact, most of my comembers said nothing to me about my temporary legal problems. The spelling-challenged graffiti painter hasn't broken out his paintbrush any more but has stopped by to chat on a couple of occasions when I've been outside. The housekeeper is back on her biweekly mission to keep my place clean and neat, and I manicure my yard with the latest state-of-the-art lawn care equipment at least once a week.

On another front, I'm cultivating a romantic interest. I've not been quick to enter the dating world since my wife passed away a couple of years ago. It probably speaks volumes about my ego, but I notice that I am physically attracted to women who are generally 20–25 years younger than me. This high standard of sorts has been mostly responsible for the fact I haven't asked even one member of the opposite sex for a date. I figure most good-looking younger women aren't interested in seeing someone who is old enough to be their father, especially if he isn't rich.

A young lady at church, Elaine, has captured my attention, and she's within ten years of my age. I noticed she is no longer wearing a wedding ring, leading me to assume she is at least separated, if not going through a divorce. She has two teenage kids, but that doesn't bother me. I'm now saying hi to her when I see her between the worship service and Sunday school. Fortunately, she also teaches in the youth department, and I've engaged her in some meaningless conversation on a couple of occasions. I suspect she knows I'm attracted to her, but I haven't made any life-changing moves yet, like asking her out to dinner.

I don't know any of her friends, other than one who I believe is a gossip. If I query this particular lady, not only Elaine, but the entire church, will know I'm interested in her. I don't think I'm ready for that yet. I've done one of those things that is embarrassing if anyone else finds out. I looked in a couple of places on the Internet to confirm her home phone number and loaded it onto my cell phone. It sounds crazy, but it makes me smile to scroll through my contacts and see her name pop up. I hope to come up with a way to approach her in the not-too-distant future. Meanwhile, I keep the ring finger on her left hand under close watch to verify her continuing probable availability.

CHAPTER 27

SATURDAY NIGHT

I enjoyed a relaxing first half of my weekend and am looking forward to a possible Elaine sighting in the morning at church. As I prepare to go to bed, I lay out the Polo shirt and slacks I'll wear in the morning. I find myself thinking about Bob Ireland less and less, but I know he still represents a future bump in my road and maybe a whole lot more.

I turn off the TV at 11:30 p.m. and let my dogs outside in the front yard. I leash them to be sure they don't run off, and still, for some unknown cosmic reason, they clearly prefer relieving themselves in front of the house as opposed to the backyard. I bring them back inside and turn off the porch light. I smile as I anticipate a restful night's sleep between my 1,000-thread-count sheets. I don't know it at this moment, but the "bump in the road" is about to get my attention once again.

ONE BLOCK AWAY

The stolen car with plates taken from another car has a clear line of sight to the Harrington house. The man behind the wheel smokes the last of a cigarette and puts it out in the ashtray. He just finished watching his target walk out of the front door of his house with his two dogs and walk around for a few minutes in the yard while they did their business. The target is now back inside his home, and the last lights upstairs went out fifteen minutes ago. The man thinks he should probably wait a little longer, but he is anxious to get this over with. He hits the kill switch to prevent the car's interior lights from coming on when he opens the door. He checks the magazine of his pistol and reinserts it into the handle. He checks the silencer. He puts the gun back in his jacket pocket. He then opens the car door quietly, smiles, and starts down the street toward the target's house.

CHAPTER 28

MONDAY: SIX MONTHS LATER

It's early May, and spring flowers and buds are in full bloom, including my favorite dogwood tree in my front yard. My life has been fairly unremarkable since the break-in back in November. My job is going well, and I still enjoy traveling from New Orleans, Louisiana, to Raleigh, North Carolina, and points in between to interview disability claimants for DPG. I consider being allowed to work out of my house and engage in extensive traveling a dream job.

As usual, on Mondays, I'm working in my home office. I have a report to dictate from a visit last week and some appointments to firm up for the week after next. I like to be scheduled for at least two weeks into the future. I plan to be finished with my dictation and study the case file that was sent to me in advance of tomorrow's field visit in Jackson, Mississippi. Thank God for Delta in Atlanta and its direct flights to and from almost anywhere.

For a moment, my thoughts drift back to the terrifying night last November. If not for my precautions, I'm sure I would have been a goner. He was long gone before the police arrived, but I have no doubt it was Bob Ireland. The local cops have no leads and, truth be told, they are probably no longer working on it. One local detective asked me if I was expecting some kind of a break-in or trouble. I told him no, but I understand why he asked the question.

Last fall, I had a state-of-the-art alarm system installed. The minute the intruder, almost certainly Ireland, broke a window on the side of the house, a silent alarm went off, and the police were notified. I heard the window break, and my dogs were barking like mad even before the intruder was inside. I remember hearing heavy footsteps coming up the staircase and my heart rate going into warp speed.

There was a lot of pounding on my bedroom door, which became more than just a bedroom door at about the same time the alarm system was set up. My bullet-resistant steel door cost over $2,000, including installation, and proved to be worth every penny I spent on it. It took four gunshots to the door handle and held tight. The police recovered the shells in a wall in the hallway and in the attic. A forensic investigation didn't identify the bullet marking pattern. It's a wonder they didn't think I was involved in drugs. They did ask me who I thought might come after me in such a way, and if I had purposely prepared to be attacked by someone. I lied and told them I had no idea who would break in, and I have nothing to hide. Wrong, of course, on both counts.

I think of the incident as a home invasion that would have ended badly except for my extreme precautions. I remember the guy who installed the door telling me I had security as impressive as most banks. And as it turned out, I needed it. One good thing came of the break-in. It convinced me that (1) Ireland is still in the country, and (2) he isn't going to leave me alone.

So I sit at my desk in my home office after dictating a report and again think of the plan I came up with a few weeks ago. I have no idea when Ireland will take another shot at me, but I'm sure it's only a matter of time. Next time, I may not be so lucky. Also, I have to consider that he'll come after me outside my home since my bedroom is a pretty effective fortress. I have only one option in my mind. I have to go on the offensive.

I gave serious consideration to going to the local police and telling them exactly what happened last year when Gayle Wade was killed. I could then ask for police protection from Ireland. This option has several possible drawbacks including legal action against me for, among other things, disposing of a murder weapon and not coming forward as an eyewitness. And if I somehow managed to avoid being locked up, would the police really be able to protect me? How long before they tired of watching my house or just quit watching altogether?

No, the only good outcome I see for myself is that Ireland be arrested, tried, and either imprisoned or executed. He has to be taken off of the streets for me to be safe and feel comfortable. I can see no other way. For this reason, I've decided to pursue this problem on my own.

CHAPTER 29

FRIDAY

A few days later, I'm back in my home office, wrapping up the week's work activities. I sign on to the Internet on my personal PC and look at something I've been checking on a near-daily basis for the past three months. The Birmingham Police have a cold cases site with unsolved crimes on it. It includes facts about unsolved murder cases and includes a picture, if available, of the victim. The photo and write-up for Gayle Wade is unchanged and reads as follows:

Victim: Gayle Wade
W/F DOB – 3/31/1971
Age at Death: 42
Date of Incident: 7/21/2013

On July, 21, 2013, Gayle Wade was at home, apparently alone. Between 12:00 a.m. and 1:30 a.m., she was shot by an unknown intruder or intruders. She was pronounced dead at the scene and had 3 gunshot wounds from 2 different guns. The victim's boyfriend, Bob Ireland, is a person of interest and is wanted for questioning.

If you have any information regarding this case, please contact Crime Stoppers at 254-1220 or Homicide at 254-4990.

I keep hoping against hope that I'll check the site and find Ireland has been arrested. I'm not certain I'm completely out of the woods if this happens, but at least I could fall asleep a lot easier. I ask myself again if I would tell the police what really happened if Ireland were picked up, and my answers vary from yes to no to maybe.

I finally pick up my home phone and decide to try a long shot in an attempt to find out what rock Ireland is hiding under. In the course of administering disability claims, the Houston home office periodically orders surveillance to take place on some claimants, both those who are receiving benefits and those who are applying for benefits. This practice is not routinely followed but can lead to some interesting findings. It's my experience that 98 percent or greater of surveillance events derive nothing of value other than to document that a claimant is remaining in his home except to walk to his mailbox or put the trash can out.

However, once in a while, surveillance discloses that a disability claimant is actually working or engaging in activities way beyond what would be expected of someone who is claiming to be sick or injured. The field representative staff is charged with being the contact persons with respect to the surveillance vendors we use across the country. They probably number in the area of fifty firms. I am familiar with six surveillance outfits and have regular contact with them to schedule surveillance events and to receive periodic updates on active assignments.

Although DPG doesn't use these vendors for purposes of finding a missing person, this type of service is offered if needed. The surveillance vendors usually refer to this service as skip tracing. I call my favorite contact person, Aaron Brown, of Hearty Investigative Services out of Nashville, Tennessee. I like working with Aaron because he is willing to always go the extra mile to service his clients and often on very short notice.

I dial Aaron's number, and he responds, "Hello."

I say, "Hi, Aaron. This is Kevin of Disability Protection Group. Do you have a minute?" He replies in the affirmative, and I continue, "This is a personal request and has no bearing on any DPG case. I'm trying to find a guy, and I know almost nothing about him except his name, and I'm not really sure about that. I'd like to try to find out where he's living. What methods do you guys use for trying to find someone who doesn't want to be found?"

Aaron replied, "Well, we have databases we check, and we'll certainly run a background check on your guy if we can verify his name and other identifying information. But the most effective way we find people is pretexting. As you know, we never pretext in a DPG case, per the instructions from your management and legal department. But I can tell you that pretexting really works. For example, we call known associates or relatives of the person and indicate we're an organization trying to find people who are due unexpected tax refunds. We also might indicate that we represent law firms who are searching for secondary beneficiaries of a rich distant relative who died with no immediate heirs. It's kind of a questionable practice, but it seems to work."

I think about what he just said for a minute and decide that I'm not concerned about playing fair and aboveboard with Ireland. I briefly tell Aaron all I know about Ireland, primarily his name and the fact he probably lived in the Birmingham area. He runs a quick database query while I wait and finds someone who might fit the bill. Aaron says this guy he found is Robert L. Ireland, and his most recent address is in Birmingham, Alabama. His date of birth is listed as August 8, 1970, and I reply that could be correct.

Aaron checks Facebook and doesn't find Ireland. He asks if I know any acquaintances, and I give him the name of Gayle Wade. I figure she won't be on Facebook or another social site. But I'm wrong. He finds a Facebook page for Gayle, and I think to myself I should have found it too before I interviewed her. He asks me to go to her Facebook page, and I do. We look at the photographs posted by Gayle before her death. I realize I'm lucky that someone didn't shut her page down after she died. And to my surprise, I see a picture I'm sure is Bob Ireland. It has the words *My love, Bob* just below it. *Oh my goodness, thank you, Gayle,* I think. I fill Aaron in on the fact that Gayle was murdered, and Ireland is a person of interest in her demise, as well as a missing person. He has no comments or questions after listening to this information.

I tell Aaron that I'm 95 percent sure this is the guy I'm looking for. He says, "Well, it's good to have a picture in case we think we find him." Aaron indicates that the electronic check on Robert L. Ireland shows several associates and relatives. He explains that this database information is frequently not 100 percent accurate, but it gives him a starting point to make calls and attempt to locate Ireland.

When I give him the go-ahead to look for Ireland, I tell him he needs to keep our arrangement confidential. He says he will, and he won't charge me for his efforts. I tell him that wouldn't be appropriate since we have a business relationship, and I'll mail him a check for $500 to begin looking. He indicates that's plenty for now, and he'll refund any unearned money, if applicable, after his investigation. I ask Aaron if he thinks he might be more likely to locate this guy than the police. He responds, "You'd be surprised how many people we locate that the police looked for and couldn't find." He then promises to keep me updated, and we end the call. I feel better now that I'm trying something to locate Ireland. Who knows, maybe I'll get lucky. The problem would then be, what do I do and where do I go from there?

CHAPTER 30

TUESDAY

I catch a 7:30 a.m. flight from Atlanta to Mobile, Alabama. I'm in town to interview a physician claiming disability due to bipolar syndrome. She's only thirty-eight years old and has been earning in excess of $400,000 a year as an orthopedic surgeon. Her claim file indicates she hasn't worked for the last two months. Her husband is an architect, and they are expecting me to arrive at their home to interview her at 11:00 a.m. (CST).

I took another quick look at her claim file during the flight. Her name is Dr. Susan Pippinger. Her husband's name is Don Pippinger. I pull into the circular driveway and am impressed by the house. It appears to be at least five thousand square feet in size, made of brick and stone, and there is an operational water fountain in the front. The property sings big bucks to me.

I ring the doorbell and wait a couple of minutes to no avail. I start walking back to my rental car so I can try to call Dr.

Pippinger on my cell phone when she finally opens the door. She is a very attractive woman with blond hair and a tanned complexion. However, she looks a little disoriented, almost as if she has been drinking. Upon closer inspection, she is wearing a tight white blouse and, it's obvious, no bra. Her slacks are black and tight. Red flags explode in my brain as I step through the door per her invitation.

She looks at me, rubs her eyes, and says, "Excuse my appearance. My medicine makes me goofy for about thirty minutes after I take it." Without trying to sound concerned, I ask her, "Is your husband here? You indicated we needed to meet today so he could be here for the interview."

She replies in a slurred voice, "No, he was called out of town on business. He won't be here."

I feel a slight surge of panic and remark, "I don't mind coming back on another day so Mr. Pippinger can be here."

She then touches my chest lightly and says, "No, that's okay. We can go ahead and talk. I'd like to get it over with." And I think to myself, *I would like to get out of here*. I decide that I'll go ahead with the interview but leave immediately if she puts her hand on me again or anything else weird occurs.

She directs me to a small couch, and I sit down on it. Instead of sitting in another chair, she chooses to sit next to me, only a couple of feet to my left. "Dr. Pippinger, can we sit at the kitchen table or the dining room table so I can take notes?" I ask. She gets up slowly and leads me to the kitchen. She takes a seat across the table from me, and this makes me feel a little better. Over the course of the next ninety minutes, Dr. Pippinger begins to talk more clearly and appears more alert.

She is able to describe, in detail, her moods swings leading from deep depressions to crazy shopping sprees in which she spends thousands of dollars.

She also shares that she stopped performing surgeries shortly before taking a leave of absence because she was either overwhelmed by the prospects of performing a procedure or she felt like superwoman and thought she could operate on patients all day long with no breaks. She cries briefly while discussing her symptoms but remains composed the rest of the time. The interview goes well, and I thank her for her time at its conclusion. We shake hands, and I feel relieved to get back to the rental car and head for the airport. I was very close to not conducting the field visit without her husband being present.

This was my first interview with a woman alone in her house since the Wade field visit, I think. And I recall, Ireland was there, so I wasn't actually alone with Wade. I decide that my reticence to enter Dr. Pippinger's house was a good thing, and I need to stay alert to possible risky situations. I breathe deeply and am again grateful that things went well during the visit. Maybe my antenna is too sensitive, but I quickly decide it's better to be safe than sorry.

Shortly after I arrive at the Mobile International Airport, my cell phone rings. I answer the call, and it's Aaron Brown of Hearty Investigative. He says, "Kevin, I may have found your man." I sit down in the gate area and ask him to continue. Brown explains, "As I told you before, our most effective way to find somebody is pretexting. As you undoubtedly know, it's also the practice that draws us the most criticism, even more that surveillance does. Since this is a personal matter and not a DPG referral, I tried it, and it seems to have paid off. There were about twenty relatives listed on the databases we searched. Their addresses are listed in most cases, and we dismissed the ones who live out of state in favor of first trying to reach the ones who live near Mr. Ireland's last known address in Birmingham.

"I'm personally handling this for you, and I made something like ten calls, reaching five people. Only one of them thought he knew Mr. Ireland, but he wasn't sure. He said if it is the right guy, he hasn't seen him for years. Then, earlier today, I hit pay dirt. I called a Mr. Tom Simonson, who lives in Hoover, Alabama. He said he knows Mr. Ireland well, as they are cousins. He wanted to know why I was trying to reach him, and I presented a scenario that I was trying to find him to inform him of unclaimed money due him from a bank. I told Mr. Simonson that I wasn't supposed to share too many details, but a long deceased relative has a modest savings account that was never closed and was willed to Mr. Ireland. I told him I work for a firm who identifies these situations and finds the lucky people due the money for a reasonable finding fee. I added that I couldn't share any more information with him due to the chance of violating Mr. Ireland's confidentiality rights. I then indicated it would be worth Mr. Ireland's efforts as the amount now exceeds $17,000 with accumulated interest over the years.

"Simonson bought my story and told me he is pretty certain that Bob could use the money. I asked him how to get in touch with him, and he said he didn't know for sure because he had to leave the area last year. I then told Simonson that I would recommend to Ireland that he give him a monetary reward for helping me when I find him. Simonson told me that he only knows his post office box number in the event he needed to reach him for something very important. I asked Simonson why he was so hard to reach, and he replied that he has some legal issues. I told Simonson that I would send Mr. Ireland a certified letter informing him of his good fortune. I also cautioned Simonson not to contact Mr. Ireland himself about this because I have to follow an evidentiary chain of discovery to be sure the funds can be released to the legal owner. Thankfully, Simonson didn't ask me to explain this as I made it up on the fly.

"He then gave me the address and asked me to be sure to explain to Ireland why he told me how to contact him. I told him I would do so and would try to get Mr. Ireland to share some of his gain with him. He told me he was sure he would, because they are good friends as well as cousins. Anyhow, I think our friend has a rental mailbox at a UPS store in San Diego, California. The address is 5705 Murano Road, San Diego, California 92126."

I look at my watch and see I still have forty-five minutes before my flight is scheduled to leave. I tell Brown, "That's great, Aaron. I can't believe you got this lead. What's your recommendation now?"

He responds, "I think we should set up one of our California associates to conduct surveillance on the UPS store. We can send him the Facebook photo of Ireland and see if he can spot him. If he shows up, we can follow him and find out where he's living."

This is about what I expected Brown to say. I tell him I'm interested in taking this thing further, but my financial situation doesn't allow me to give him carte blanche on running up my bill. Brown then offers, "I didn't spend the entire $500 you paid so far on research and phone calls. Our going rate for surveillance is $650 per day. If you are willing to spend up to another $1,500, we can commit to three full days of surveillance. Of course, if it rains or something, we'll back off in order to use the time wisely. And if we find him before using all of the approved hours, you'll be due a refund. What do you say?"

I think about how badly I want to find this guy. My life is overshadowed by my recurring fear that I'll walk around a corner or walk out of a restaurant and find myself staring into the barrel of a gun held by Bob Ireland. I decide quickly and answer, "Okay, let's do it. But I would like it if your guy uses his head and breaks off surveillance if it seems unlikely he'll show up due to weather or whatever. Also, I would suggest that the observations take place between 9:00 a.m. and 3:00 p.m. That way, we might squeeze in a fourth day if needed."

Brown agrees with this proposed schedule and indicates he can get this thing started by Friday. I also suggest that he not observe on Sunday, even if the public has access to their rented mailboxes. He says he'll give instructions to not work the case on Sunday and tells me not to worry about sending any more money until it's time to settle up. I thank him and ask if these mailbox places notify box renters when they receive mail. He answered that many do, and he plans to send a piece of junk mail to Ireland to, hopefully, initiate a visit to the UPS store. He promises to keep me informed, thanks me again, and hangs up.

As I wait for the announcement to board my flight to Atlanta, I think to myself this might be a waste of money. But if it works, I'll be in a position to consider several courses of action instead of feeling like I have no control.

CHAPTER 31

SUNDAY

I'm walking from the main church facility to the youth building between services when I see Elaine walking toward me. She solicits the usual chemical reaction from me as I become nervous and think, once again, how attractive she is. I try to work up the nerve to stop her and initiate a conversation. As I get closer, she smiles, and my heart and courage dissolve. Then she drops a packet of papers right in front of me. Is this providence or did she do it on purpose, I wonder.

She is already kneeling to pick the information up, and I go to one knee to assist her. She looks at me, her face only inches from mine, and says "Why, thanks, Kevin."

It seems like there is nothing or no one else in the universe but me and her at this moment, and I enjoy the feeling. "You're welcome," I say and add, "Are you doing all right?" Not the cleverest opening line but at least I was able to talk and not slobber on her.

She stands, and I hand her the papers I picked up. She takes them—and am I imagining this?—her hand touches mine and then lingers for a few seconds. Apparently, I'm smitten because I'm certain I give her a goofy grin and then try to cut if off before she thinks I'm more than mildly retarded. She then says, "How are you getting along? It's been a couple of years since your wife died, hasn't it?"

I'm simultaneously thrilled she's talking to me and horrified that she mentioned my deceased wife. I respond with a brilliant remark worthy of literary recognition, "Yes." *Doggone it,* I think to myself, *don't talk in one-syllable words to this goddess.* So I add, "That's right." *Great,* I think, *two words.* If Ireland showed up right now, I think I'd grab his gun and point it at my own stupid skull.

Elaine then comes closer to me, and I think I'm about to evaporate and float away. She says, "I hope you're doing okay. I think you're a pretty good guy."

My first thought is, *Don't you read the newspaper?* But I manage to respond, "I think you're more than okay, Elaine." Kind of weak but the best I can muster without passing out at her feet.

I then take the biggest risk I can remember since the Wade interview and ask her, "Would you like to go to dinner with me sometime?" She looks momentarily puzzled, and I hope she doesn't break out laughing. But instead, to my incredible relief, she answers, "Sure. Give me a call."

Is that it? I think. Isn't the ground supposed to start shaking while the orchestra plays "The Phantom of the Opera" in the background? I grin sheepishly and tell her, "I sure will." *Wow,*

I think, *three whole words. She'll think I was on the college debate team or something.*

She smiles again and walks in the opposite direction I'm heading. My steps seem lighter, and I tell myself not to whoop and holler out loud. I have a lot of questions I'd like to ask her, and when we settle on a dinner date, I should get the chance. What a great day, I think. But that will change in a couple of hours.

2:00 P.M.

After having lunch with some church friends, I'm headed home and thinking about taking my dogs for a walk. After parking my car in the garage, I change clothes and hear my home phone ring. I pick it up and say, "Hello."

There's a few seconds of silence, and I start to hang up when I hear, "That's one helluva bedroom door you have there, Harrington." I freeze in disbelief. It's Ireland! I quickly check my caller ID, and it says, *private name.*

"What do you want?" I ask him.

He replies, "I want you dead. I'm not making any more mistakes with you. I should have offed you when I had the chance. I know you have kids, and I've found out where they live."

My blood freezes while I process this threat. I can only say, "Okay, what is it you want?"

"You," he says. "I want you. You're a major pain in my ass because you can rat on me whenever you want to. For all I know, you may have talked to the cops about me already."

I think carefully before saying, "I haven't yet, but this call may change my mind."

He then says, "Look, I'm betting you're a standup guy. You got two kids, a nice house, and a job with that hotsy totsy company. If you meet me in person and pay me $10,000, I promise I'll leave the country, and you'll never hear from me again. And your kids will be safe."

I immediately know that if I were to meet with him under these circumstances, he'd kill me and take the money. But I need to buy some time, so I say, "That may be doable. But I'll need some time to raise that kind of money."

He responds, "Sure, Mr. Bigshot. You got two weeks. I'll be back in touch at that time, and I may need you to come out west to meet with me."

I think to myself, *We're probably closing in on you, lowlife.* I then tell him, "Mr. Ireland, I'll need at least two weeks to get that kind of money out of my retirement fund. Also, I travel for my job across several states. I think you should have my cell phone number so you won't think I'm ignoring you if you call here and I don't get back to you real quick." I'm surprised at my calmness in talking to him. I feel like I'm watching myself in a movie dealing with this murderer.

Then I take the offensive, "Look, Mr. Ireland. I have something to tell you. If you harm so much as a hair on the heads of either of my children, I'll run you down and kill you with my bare hands. And if I'm not around to do this, I'll have someone else ready to take my place. It won't matter where you are. You'll be dealt with."

I pause and hope I haven't made a mistake by getting tough when Ireland says, "Okay, I hear you. I understand you love your kids. You have my word that nothing will happen to them before I get the money or after I get it. You hear me?"

I feel some relief at this quasi-concession and say, "Good enough."

He then snarls, "If you cross me in this thing, there'll be hell to pay from you and your family." I ignore this and give him my cell phone number so he can reach me more reliably. I ask him to repeat the number, which he does.

I then say, "For right now, don't call me or anyone I know. I'll expect to hear from you in two weeks and no sooner on my cell phone. Understand?" He says he does, and I end the call.

I sit on the couch and put my head in my hands. It seems like an eternity ago, not a few hours, when Elaine agreed to take a chance on going to dinner with me. I think to myself that it'll be some time before I call her, if I'm in a position to do so at all.

I lay out my options in my mind. I can go to Detective Skirvin and get his help if I choose to do so. I see no way to do this without telling him everything. This doesn't seem like a great idea since I'm probably closer to finding Ireland than they are. If I choose to leave the police out of this, I have to be sure I can take of Ireland. I also have to do something to get my kids out of harm's way. I don't trust Ireland not to go after them in the interim period when I'm supposed to be rounding up the $10,000.

I come to the conclusion that I'm going to have to deal with Ireland in about two weeks or, hopefully, sooner if Hearty Investigative can find him. I'd obviously prefer to find him first and surprise him in lieu of walking into a situation he sets up. I tell myself I don't think he's particularly smart, but he's extremely dangerous. I get out a piece of paper and a pen and begin jotting down some options and possible plans. I take time to pray, believing I'll need all the help I can get.

CHAPTER 32

MONDAY

I t's the first of my usual work-at-home days, but I have no time for anything work related today. The first order of business is to take care of the safety of my kids. I decide not to level with them completely because I don't want to scare them to death. I feel reasonably secure that Ireland won't move against either of them before he has a chance to extort $10,000 from me.

I find Peaceful Haven on the Internet, a bed-and-breakfast in Hot Springs, Arkansas. I have vacationed in this area in the past; it's close to Branson, Missouri, a sort of hillbilly and blue grass entertainment version of Disney World. I call the management at Peaceful Haven and tell them I need two rooms for a week on very little notice. After giving them a $1,000 deposit on my MasterCard, they agree to hold two rooms over the next two weeks for any seven days I require. Now, I only have to convince my kids to drop everything and travel to Hot Springs.

As I dial my daughter's number, I hope it won't seem too coincidental that the bed-and-breakfast is approximately halfway between Lubbock, Texas, and the Chicago area where her brother lives. I tell her I won a contest through a trade magazine and have the opportunity to use two rooms at Peaceful Haven for seven days. The only catch, I tell her, is that the days must be used during the next two weeks.

She asks me when I found out I won, and I respond it was over the weekend. Thankfully, she requests no more details and asks if her boyfriend can come with her. Normally, this would at least irritate me, but I say, "Sure, bring Jessie." Since she's not in class during the summer and her work schedule is light, she says she's pretty sure she can go. She promises to let me know later in the day.

Next, I call my son, the asphalt sales manager. He's home this morning but preparing to leave on a sales trip. I relate the contest story to him and ask if he and his wife can make it to Hot Springs within the next week. He tells me that it's great that I won, but I should also go to the resort and enjoy myself. I tell him I'm especially busy right now and booked solid for the next three weeks, but I want him and his sister to take advantage of the opportunity. He puts the phone down briefly and speaks with his wife. He comes back on the line and says he and Jenny will leave for Arkansas on Friday morning. I tell him to check in under my name and that everything is taken care of. He thanks me and then tells me he loves me. I say good-bye and hang up.

As soon as I put the phone down, my daughter calls and tells me she and Jessie are going to leave on Saturday. I tell her that her brother and sister-in-law will beat them there by a day. She also tells me she loves me, and I start to feel really guilty. After I hang up, I cry for a minute and pray that I'm doing the right thing. I think my kids are safe for the next two weeks, but the fact they'll be out of town the second week of this time period comforts me a little.

It's about noon and I call Aaron Brown of Hearty Investigative. I hope to high heaven he has some good news for me. And miraculously, he does. He reports that Friday was a bust but, on Saturday morning, the investigator spotted someone who looked like Ireland going to the mailbox area. He confirmed that this guy went to the correct box number as supplied by the cousin, Simonson. He continued that the individual removed some mail, glanced at it, and threw it away.

Brown continued, "Our investigator checked the trash can and managed to retrieve the stuff our suspect threw away. There were two pieces of mail, Kevin. One was the junk mail I sent, and it was addressed to resident. But the other was a postcard from Simonson addressed to a Mr. Ireland. Our man read it to me over the phone, and it appears it was written and mailed before I spoke to him. It didn't say anything other than a general how're-you-doing message.

"Frankly, our investigator made a mistake and let the guy get away unobserved when he went for the items in the trash can. I told him he'd really screwed up by not following him. I was going to call you earlier this morning, but the investigator called me first. He set up outside the UPS store early today because he found out that the mail is distributed to the boxes early because the servicing post office is only a block down the street. Well, our man came back in, but there was nothing in his box. This time, our guy followed him back to an apartment complex about a mile from Pacific Beach. It's called Cedar Pointe Apartments, and our investigator said he went directly to Apartment 3B."

I think to myself, *This is great! Maybe I've found him.* "Can you find out who the apartment is rented to?" I ask.

Brown replied, "I've already run it through the database, and this unit is rented by a Ms. Peggy Goldson for $950 a month. For San Diego, that's a cheap price, so I'm guessing it's a studio apartment or something."

I then ask, "Can you find out anything about Ms. Goldson?"

He replies that one of his associates is working on that angle right now. Brown then tells me, "And there's something else, Kevin. Our investigator took some good video of this guy. I'm sending it to you right now. I hope you can verify whether or not or this is who you're looking for."

Wow, I think, *this is great*. Briefly, I think about what I'll do if it's not Ireland. My only option then will be to meet him on his terms and that might require me to bring in the local police or the Birmingham authorities to help me. I'd like to avoid that if possible. Less than a minute later, my PC chimes that an e-mail has been received. I check it and see it's from Hearty. I open the e-mail and see a large attachment. I open it and watch as a video initializes before my eyes. I look and blink twice before looking again. I'm watching Bob Ireland walking the streets of San Diego, California, only a few hours ago. Hallelujah!

CHAPTER 33

TUESDAY

I'm so wired about finding Ireland that I can barely concentrate on my job as a field representative. Fortunately, I only have an appointment with a local claimant today and don't have to worry about fighting traffic to the airport and being gone overnight or for all day. I drive to Buford, Georgia, and talk to a factory worker who broke his leg. I find it difficult to listen to him and write down the salient points he shares with me. I'll dictate the report later and may have to call the claimant back if I can't make sense of my notes.

I arrive back home at 11:30 a.m. and find that Aaron Brown of Hearty has left a message. He asks that I call him back, and I do so immediately. He answers on the second ring and tells me he has some background on Ms. Goldson, who Ireland is apparently staying with. He begins, "She is thirty years old and was born in Paducah, Kentucky. She is twice divorced and has one kid. Her first husband has custody of the boy, who is eleven years old. She is a licensed driver in California and is the registered owner of a 2002 Toyota Celica. She has been in trouble with the law in the past for possession of a controlled substance. She's also had two speeding tickets and one moving violation over the last seven years."

Brown hesitates and then tells me, "Kevin, we made a pretext call to her apartment yesterday, and your guy answered—"

Before he could say anything, I blurted out, "Oh no, you didn't tip him off, did you?"

He responds, "No, I don't think so. I told our San Diego office that they need to sit tight on this unless I give further instructions. But anyway, one of the female staff in San Diego called and said she was trying to reach Ms. Goldson. Your guy acted put out and told her she can reach her at Show Stoppers before he hung up. The San Diego office checked the Internet, and apparently, there is a local strip club that's full name is Baby Doll Show Stoppers. Do you want us to check this out for you?"

I think for a second and reply, "No, I don't think so. I know where he's living, and it doesn't matter whether or not he's living with a stripper." I then tell Brown that I'm happy with the results he delivered, and he can send me a final bill. He estimates it will be about $2,000 less the $500 I've already paid. We exchange good-byes, and he promises to help me if I decide I want Hearty to reopen the case.

This development from Brown has completely captured my attention, and the chances of me doing any work for my employer the rest of today is slim to none. I think of my options, which seem few. I know I have to take Ireland off of the street, but what is the best way to do this and keep myself from getting in trouble? I think again about the threat made by Ireland against my kids. One thing's for sure. He's going down one way or another, even if I have to go down with him.

CHAPTER 34

WEDNESDAY

At 2:00 a.m., I wake up with a start. A strange idea has occurred to me that I need to follow up on soon. I can't go back to sleep. I'm so affixed to this sudden notion. It's a real long shot, but if it pays off, I might have a powerful card in my hand. I go over and over the short conversation with Ireland last Sunday. I replay every word in my head, and I'm convinced of one thing—he never mentioned or alluded to the tape recorder I had with me the night of the murder. There's a chance it's lying in the woods somewhere. A plan forms in my head.

At 9:00 a.m., I call my boss, Doug Wills, and tell him I woke up sick this morning. He says he's sorry to hear this and that I need to get some rest so I'll feel better. After thanking him for his concern, I tell him I'm sorry I can't fly to Charlotte, North Carolina, later this morning. I advise him that I'll call the claimant and reschedule the field visit in the future. He says this is fine and wishes me a quick recovery. I feel a little guilty being untruthful, but I tell myself this is about my future and the well-being of my kids.

After cancelling my appointment with the claimant, I contact the corporate travel vendor and let them know I won't be making the flight today. This is not a rare occurrence from a company standpoint, and they assure me they will cancel my flight and car rental. They tell me to contact them when I'm ready to reschedule the trip.

Okay, I think to myself, *I'm free for the day and no one knows my agenda. And*, I affirm to myself, *my agenda is to go to the woods near to the murder scene and find my tape recorder.* I'm excited and hope that giving a day to this activity won't hurt me in the long run. I think that Ireland has no reason to bolt, so there should be no shortcomings to taking this trip.

At 9:45 a.m., I depart from Alpharetta in my TrailBlazer. I tell myself it's less nerve-racking to drive to and hopefully return from Helena during daylight hours as opposed to my previous night time adventure. Since I'm supposed to be sick and plan to return this evening, I quickly take my dogs outside and leave them some food. I don't engage the services of my dog sitter, having already told her I don't need her today after all.

I make good time and pull into the same hiding spot where I left my other car parked several months ago. I'm wearing a camouflage jacket, matching pants, boots, and a baseball cap. I'm carrying a World War II Japanese rifle that was cleaned and polished by a gun shop in Alpharetta. It has no firing pin and is merely a prop today. It was brought back to America by my deceased father-in-law who served in the Philippines as a US Marine. It's spent the last fifteen years in the corner of my bedroom, gathering dust. Now, I'm glad I didn't have it put in a gun case as was my original plan.

I walk down the cul-de-sac toward the murder site. There's a For Sale sign in the front yard, and the house looks empty. I notice the old Camaro that was parked in the driveway is gone. I enter the woods about where I think I entered several months ago. Nothing looks familiar. I walk for an hour and decide I'll be lucky to just find my way back. Then I see something I think I remember—the bush where I tried to hide! I look closer, and I'm sure this is the same bush I stayed under for a few minutes before nearly being caught and shot at the first time.

Energized, I decide which side of the bush I probably exited and walk in that direction. After three hours, I admit to myself that I'm definitely lost and very hungry. I think to myself I'd like to find the house I came upon under construction that night and look around there since I passed out on the street in front of it. I decide to try to find a road and then work my way back to my car. As I walk around a tree, I freeze. An old guy is walking his dog and coming toward me. *Maybe he can help me*, I think.

"Hi," I say as he walks up to me.

"Hello to you, sir," he replies. He asks me if I'm hunting, and I shake my head in the affirmative. "That's funny," he says, "because the only game hunters go after here is deer, and the season doesn't open for another two months."

Dang, I think to myself, *why did I have to run into a smart old guy?* I scramble for an answer and say weakly, "Actually, I'm just checking these woods out for a hunting trip this fall."

He grins and says, "Is that why you're carrying an old Jap rifle?"

I think I'd feel better If I was caught kissing my best friend's wife and admit, "Well, I'm not really hunting, or checking out the area for a hunting trip for that matter." He looks at me with a wry grin and waits. I continue, "I'm trying to look like I belong out here while I look for a house I found several months ago. It was under construction late last year, and there was a small muddy pond behind it. It was located on a cul-de-sac as I remember it."

He continues to stare at me, and I remark, "Look, I'm not up to anything illegal or anything like that. I'm just trying to find something I lost that may be near that house, although it's a real long shot."

"Well," he says, "why didn't you say so in the first place? I'm still not convinced you're not some kind of weirdo, dressed up like a hunter with a seventy some -year-old gun, but I can't imagine anyone making up a story like that, so it must be the truth. I think I know where that house is because there's very little residential building going on out here."

I ask him if he can tell me how to find the house he thinks I'm looking for, and he responds in the affirmative. I then take a chance and ask if he can help me get back to my car at the corner of the street Ms. Wade lived on. He says he can do that too, and I follow him out of the woods and reenter the world of those who know where they are. When I'm close to my car, the old guy gives me detailed directions to the house.

Twenty minutes and three wrong turns later, I'm turning down Lost Forest Lane, most aptly named in my humble opinion. I drive a mile and a half and turn left. I come upon a solitary new house on a cul-de-sac with a For Sale sign in front of it. I note that it's the same realty company trying to sell the house Wade was killed in. I can't tell for sure if it the same house since I was in panic mode the time I may have been here earlier. I park the car and decide to leave my impotent gun in the car.

I walk around the house to the backyard, and a shiver goes up my spine. I'm certain that's the pond I ran into on that night. It looks as muddy now as it appeared to be then. The house is now landscaped, which I think is not good for me. This means that heavy machinery was used to pile up dirt and debris, smooth it out, and then plant grass seed or lay sod. Dang it!

With no good idea of how to proceed, I walk down to the pond and try to retrace my steps that night. I remember I landed with a huge thump when I came flying out of the woods into the shallow water. I'm pretty sure I came out of the thicket I see near the edge of the pond about twenty feet from me. I examine the edge and see some footprints coming out of it. Is it possible that those are my footprints from months ago? I think, probably not, when something catches my eye about ten feet from the water's edge. I do a double take and approach something shining in the late afternoon sun. My hopes are dashed when I see it's a crushed Diet Coke can. Damn, I say to myself. Then I reach down, pick up the can, and find my recorder directly underneath. I kneel, sobbing, for about five minutes. Then I chastise myself, realizing I need to keep it together because I have no idea if it still works or if the recording is still on it and intact.

I pull into my driveway at about 9:45 p.m. What a day, I think. On the trip home, I tried to turn on the digital recorder, but it was dead. No surprise, lying outside for several months. I enter the house through the garage and am greeted by two dogs with full bladders. I let them into the backyard and go to my junk drawer below my hardly used steak knife set. I find a package with three AAA batteries and open it. I put one of the fresh batteries in the back side of the recorder and reinsert the cover.

I hesitate for a second and say a short prayer that the device still works. I push the power button, and the device seems to power up. The screen indicates there is one recording. I push the play button and heave a sigh of relief as I hear Ireland and Gayle Wade arguing. "I've got it!" I say out loud.

CHAPTER 35

THURSDAY

9:00 A.M.

I have a plan formulated since I found the digital recorder, and with some luck, I may be able to pull it off in the next 3–4 days. First, I need some information. I go into my home office and place a call to Aaron Brown of Hearty Investigative. I thank him again for his company's stellar work. I tell him I'm trying to identify a licensed private investigator in San Diego who is well-regarded, has been in business for at least ten years, and is willing to work under unusual circumstances. I add that this person also needs to be available tomorrow and on the weekend. Aaron says he'll check with the local Hearty staff in San Diego and Los Angeles and get back to me as soon as possible. He reminds me that they are three hours behind us and their offices aren't open yet. I tell him I look forward to hearing from him at his earliest convenience and hang up.

Next, I look at my work schedule again. Good gosh! I didn't cancel an appointment for today. I was so caught up in making time to drive to Helena to look for the recorder yesterday that I forgot I had scheduled to stay overnight and conduct a second field visit today. I was supposed to meet this individual at a Waffle House Restaurant at 11:00 a.m. I pull my referral sheet and call him on the phone. I apologize, informing him I woke up sick yesterday. We agree to speak next week and reschedule our meeting. I fire up my PC and take a quick look at the corporate travel site. They were sharp enough to have cancelled my hotel reservation last night even though we didn't discuss it.

Now, I get back to the matter at hand. I sign onto the Delta Airlines website and make arrangements for a flight from Atlanta to San Diego for this afternoon. I put this flight on hold and have four hours to confirm it, or it will automatically cancel. I also use some Marriott points and reserve myself a room at a Fairfield Inn in San Diego near downtown. I reserve the next three nights and hope I get lucky and don't need all of them. I go to my bedroom and pack a suitcase with an extra pair of tennis shoes, three golf shirts, two pairs of shorts, and three pairs of slacks. I use the rest of the room to put in underwear, socks, toiletries, and my GPS. I call my dog sitter, Pat, and tell her I have to go out of town and may not return until Monday. She agrees to come over this evening and stay at the house with my dogs. I believe I'm all ready.

I know I'm creating a paper trail to California, but I don't care. Things will work out, or I'll have to go another route. That my whereabouts the next few days will be documented is the least of my worries. At 11:15 a.m., my phone rings. It's Aaron. He gives me the name of a private investigator with fifteen years of experience and says she's feisty, according to the Hearty staff in San Diego. Aaron also indicated the staff called her receptionist, and she's available beginning this afternoon through Sunday. He added that the Hearty manager told him he'd want her with him if he was in a tight situation. This sounds like just the kind of person I need.

I check the phone number I wrote down and dial it. The receptionist puts me through promptly, and I hear, "This is Emily Keeker. How can I help you?"

I respond, "Ms. Keeker, my name is Kevin Harrington, and I live outside of Atlanta, Georgia. I'm set up to come to San Diego this afternoon, and I need your services for the next 2–3 days. I think I can be there about four, your time."

Keeker says, "May I ask what this is about?"

I hesitate for a second because I don't want to run her off. "It's about locating a guy and then helping him get arrested."

She retorts, "I don't like to make arrangements or agreements when I'm not sure what I'm getting into."

I tell her, "I understand your concern. Let me meet you in your office later today. I'll give you all the details and answer any questions you might have. Then you can tell me yes or no. Can we go this route?"

She is silent for a short time and indicates, "Okay, but if I don't want to get involved, it's not going to matter to me that you flew all the way here to talk to me."

I respond, "Fair enough. See you at about four." She gives me her office address and promises to be there when I arrive. We end the call. I immediately call Delta, confirm my flight, and pay for it with my credit card. I feel like I'm about to walk across a super high tightrope, and in fact, that may be an accurate assessment.

I make a copy of the murder recording on another handheld digital recorder and put it in the side pocket of my suitcase. I eat a quick lunch and throw my bag in the car. I drive to the airport and park in a covered space at my usual off-site parking service. I can use my frequent parking points to pay the charge when I return. I board the flight and settle in for a 4–5 hour flight. I'm upgraded to first class because of my frequent flyer status and enjoy a decent meal. I also get a couple of hours of sleep, which I always do when I fly.

I deplane in San Diego after an interesting approach in which the plane seems to be flying between tall downtown buildings. I collect my rental car, again paid for with points, and enter Keeker's address in my GPS. I arrive at her office near Old Town at about 4:15 p.m. I go into the waiting area, and there is no one behind the reception window. The décor looks professional, sort of like a lawyer's office, with leather furniture and dark paneled walls. I knock lightly on the window and hear someone yell, "Come on back, unless you're a bill collector."

I go through the only door besides the entrance and find a small hallway. It leads to an office with a closed door. I knock and hear, "Come in." I open the door and get my first look at Emily Keeker. She looks to be about forty years old, is stunningly attractive, and is dressed to the nines. She has medium-length brown hair with a barrette to keep it out of her bright blue eyes. She is dressed in a red business suit with a tight skirt that shows her nice build. She looks as if she has lean, muscled shoulders. She looks up from her desk and says, "You Harrington?"

I confirm I am, and we shake hands. I notice she has a small gun holstered in the interior left pocket of her jacket. This, I think, is good. She dispenses with small talk and formalities and states, "Okay, tell me your story."

And for the first time ever, I tell my story from beginning to end, leaving out nothing. It takes about fifteen minutes.

When I'm done, she sits there for a minute and remarks, "That's a heck of a tale. I'd say you're lucky to still be in one piece."

Thanks for telling me what I already know, I think.

She resumes, "I can't believe you found the recorder. Did you bring it with you?"

"I have a copy of the recording in my bag. The original recorder's at my house," I reply. She requests that I go to my car and get the copy so she can listen to it. When it plays through, which takes, to my surprise, only about a minute, she asks, "Was that you screaming no?"

I respond in the affirmative, and she tells me, "You're really lucky he didn't shoot you, too."

I lean back in the chair and stretch my arms outward. She looks at me and says, "What do you have in mind?" I tell her my tentative plan, and she sits back and scratches her pretty head. "This could backfire, and one or both of us could get hurt," she says softly. I ask her if she can come up with something better, and she retorts, "How about turning everything over to the police?"

I'm ready for that question and fire back, "I found this guy in less than a week, although I used an investigative firm to do it. They've been looking for him for months. I'm not sure I trust any police department to close this deal. Plus, he's threatened me and my children, and I want to be sure he's taken off the street."

She crinkles her nose at me and replies, "I think I can help you. My fee is $1,000 a day plus expenses, with a deposit of $2,000 up front." I ask if she can take a credit card, and she replies, "Of course." She takes my card into another room and runs it through her card reader making her instantly $2,000 richer.

Surprisingly, she has no objections to my plan. I thought for sure she would make some different suggestions, if not outright changes. We agree to meet tomorrow morning in her office at 7:00 a.m. She reminds me to bring the written report and the video from Hearty Investigative with me.

CHAPTER 36

FRIDAY

I wake up at 8:30 a.m. according to my watch and panic. Then I remember I'm on the West Coast, and its only 5:30 a.m. here. I put on a pair of shorts, a tee shirt, and a pair of tennis shoes and run through the streets of Pacific Beach and Ocean Beach. It's about sixty degrees, perfect running weather. This is a beautiful area, I think to myself, and I can see why Southern California is such a big draw to the young and old alike.

I return, shower, shave, and get dressed in slacks, a golf shirt, and the casual shoes I wore during yesterday's flight. I eat a light continental breakfast in the lobby of the hotel and head to Keeker's office. I arrive ten minutes early and see one car in the parking lot, a late model BMW. Must be her car, I presume.

The front door is open, and I walk directly to her office. She's behind her desk, reading something. She's wearing a pantsuit today and looks even better, if that's possible. It's navy blue, and she has on a white sheer blouse. I have trouble taking my eyes off of her, and she says, "Down, Fido." I feel myself blush and apologize. Oddly enough, I think briefly about Elaine and remember I haven't called her yet. I'm glad I didn't give her a deadline to hear from me.

Keeker takes the DVD made by Hearty and plays it several times. She stops it on Ireland's face several times before asking me, "Are you sure this is him?"

I firmly reply, "Without a doubt."

She then reads the report compiled by Hearty and remarks, "He's living with a stripper, huh? The American dream, I guess. She's probably working nights, so she'll be at the apartment sleeping during the day. We'll need to wait until your man leaves to go someplace." I nod in agreement with this statement.

"We can watch the apartment complex and try to follow Ireland when he leaves it," she explains and adds, "This can get real boring." I think to myself that I need to keep my eyes off of Keeker and on the apartment complex when we find a place to observe the area. She reaches into one of her desk drawers and pulls out an M&P9 9mm handgun. She hands it to me and says, "Put this in your pocket just in case. It's loaded. I did some research, and Georgia residents don't need a license of any kind to carry a concealed weapon. Ergo, you don't need one here either." She also hands me a pair of plastic restraints and instructs, "Keep these in your back pocket. I'm armed and have a set of handcuffs. I want to be sure we don't find ourselves lacking the equipment to handle this guy."

By now, it's seven thirty, and Keeker looks to be in no hurry to leave the office as she pours herself another cup of coffee.

She looks at me with those penetrating eyes and says, "Take it easy, bulldog. I'm betting this guy doesn't get up until at least 9:00 a.m." I ask her if we need to go over our plan before we drive to the stripper's apartment, and she responds, "Not really, because we're probably going to have to improvise on the run. I don't want you having a certain idea in your head if it doesn't fit the situation we find ourselves in. Make sense?" I shake my head up and down but am uneasy about stepping into this mess now that it's about to happen, even though this beauty queen comes highly recommended.

Just after 9:00 a.m., we pull into the parking lot of a bagel shop across the street from the apartment complex Ireland is most likely living in. There are a lot of people on the street, as it's a trendy area with a lot of shops and restaurants. I calculate that I've already incurred about $200 in expenses for my pretty gum shoe, which makes me wonder if this whole thing will pay off. Keeker's BMW is parked in the middle of the lot, affording us a view of the front of the complex. This is fine because there is a fence separating the complex from the adjacent property behind it, effectively making the street side the only point of egress for the tenants.

Shortly after 10:00 a.m., Ireland walks out of the apartment complex and into the bagel shop where we're parked. I experience a jolt, like I'm having an out-of-body experience! I figure he must want breakfast. I wonder where he gets his money and speculate that he could be living off his girlfriend's earnings. As we wait for him to come out, Keeker says, "I don't want to confront him here and now. There're too many people around, and one of them might try to help him." We're parked on the second row of the lot from the front door, and a car in front of us pulls out.

Just then, Ireland exits the shop with a white bag in one hand. He looks directly at us and zeros in on me. I'm frozen and can't look away. He registers a surprised look on his face that then turns angry. He takes the time to give me the finger before running across the street to the apartment complex. I look at Keeker and ask, caustically, "Think he recognized me?"

She actually smiles and answers, "Maybe."

To my complete surprise, Keeker pulls out of the lot and drives back to her office. "What are you doing?" I practically yell at her. "He's going to take off, and we'll never find him."

All she said was, "Maybe not." I'm trying to stay quiet so I won't blurt out something I'll regret later as she executes a NASCAR driver's move off a banked turn and slides into her parking lot. We run into her office, and she pulls out a small PC from her desk. She fires it up and opens a program I can't identify from my vantage point.

Then I recognize what I'm looking at. It's a GPS-type screen with streets identified and different colored lines. There is also a yellow triangle that is moving from street to street on the grid. She announces, "I'm pretty sure that's our guy right there. And it looks like he may be headed for I-5."

My brain is feeling overloaded, and this isn't computing with me, so I ask, "How could that be? I mean, how can his car show up on this screen, even if it is his car?"

She responds, "I started earning the fee you're paying me last night. I followed Ireland and his squeeze to Show Stoppers for her pole dancing gig. Ireland drove the car and stayed for the eight-hour shift while Ms. Goldson shuddered and undulated. I put a GPS tracker beacon under her rear bumper, figuring these bottom-feeders don't own two cars. I know Ms. American Woman doesn't go on until 11:00 p.m. according to the sign on the door to the strip club, so I'd guess this is our boy or our boy and his slut."

Goodness, I think, *she has such a way with words.* "I'd feel better if we could verify this is Ireland," I remark.

"Your wish is my command, captain," she replies. "So let's take a leisurely drive wherever this lowlife takes us. I feel pretty sure this is him." I do too, but I say nothing as Keeker grabs the small PC and a car adapter to power it. We walk briskly to her car and get inside. She connects the PC to the power outlet, and the screen pops up in bright colors. As she predicted, the yellow triangle is headed north on I-5 toward Anaheim and Los Angeles.

We hit the freeway and settle into a smooth 80-mile-per-hour cruise. I suggest we try to catch up to the car, and she tells me to play the quiet game. How nice. I briefly consider trying out my plastic restraints on her, but I imagine she'd clean my clock before I got too far. I then venture, "What will we do if this, somehow, isn't Ireland?" She hesitates before responding, "I guess I'll think about giving you a partial refund." I decide I'll try the quiet game since it's not as aggravating as talking to my cute chauffer.

CHAPTER 37

After a couple of hours, we're nearing the Los Angeles city limits. Keeker is maintaining a following distance of about a half mile and comments, "We probably should have grabbed your rental car since he's seen my BMW. We'll have to be careful."

Ireland, at least I hope it's him, exits at Marietta Street and turns left on Whittier Boulevard. He goes about two blocks and enters a parking lot of a place called Show Stoppers II. Well, well, another strip club. We park across the street from the parking lot and watch the car. In a few minutes, the driver's door opens, and Ms. Goldson gets out. My heart rate accelerates as I think we've followed the wrong person. Then to my great relief—and fear—Ireland gets out of the passenger side of the car.

They give the appearance that they are not in any hurry and walk arm in arm like they don't have a care in the world. They saunter across the parking lot and enter the club. I ask Keeker, "Think she's working in there today?"

She replies, "I doubt it. It's only 1:30 p.m."

That's true, I think. "So do we just wait here?" I ask, and she says, "Maybe."

Good, I feel better when I know what she's thinking. "Any other nice surprises you've kept from me like the GPS tracker?" I ask.

"Probably not," she says.

"That's probably good," I snap back.

She looks at me, smiles, and suggests, "Save that nasty for later, tiger."

By 4:30 p.m., we're both tired of waiting. We talk about my plan again and decide it may be time to force our hand in this matter. We enter the club, and it's everything I was afraid it would be. It smells of beer, urine, cigarette smoke, and desperation. There are about 10–12 customers, and as soon as we walk in, their attention diverts from the fifteen-year-old on the pole to Keeker. Smart choice, I think.

We spot Ireland sitting in a corner with a drunk-appearing dancer, probably Goldson, I surmise. We walk straight up to him as we'd decided to do before we came in. I stand behind Keeker—how brave of me—and she says to him, "Stand up, choir boy."

Choir boy? I think. *Where does she come up with these witty words?* Then things turn serious.

Ireland stands and pulls the largest knife I've ever seen. It looks to be the size of a sword. Keeker shouts at him, "This is a gun fight, dumbass," and draws her Sig Sauer out of her pocket. It gets Ireland's attention. I put my hand on the gun in my pocket and pray I don't have to show it.

Then, in the blink of an eye, the slut girlfriend demonstrates she's not as wasted as she appears to be and brings her drink glass down hard on Keeker's gun. It fires as it clatters to the floor. Ireland seems stunned for a moment but then dives for the Sig. I am terrified but retain enough composure to jump on him and keep him from reaching the slowly spinning gun. He reacts violently and elbows me in the nose. I get mad, and despite the blinding pain and gushing blood from my probably broken nose, I grab his hair and bang his forehead into the floor. It makes a sickening thud.

Meanwhile, Keeker punches Ireland's squeeze, and she goes down and then out, like a light. She recovers her gun and points it at Ireland's face, saying, "How do you like it? Sliced or diced?" I think to myself that she's earned the $2,000 already. She's in a class by herself. She invites Ireland to stand and them kicks him in the ribs when he hesitates. He starts to rise slowly.

I'm holding my bleeding nose when major trouble appears. I no longer wonder where this establishment's muscle is. I see a huge gorilla running across the dark room, and he's headed right for Keeker's back. I realize she doesn't see him or the black jack-looking thing in his right hand.

Possibly due to some form of primal survival instinct, I pull out my gun and fire twice into the ceiling. Dancers, I assume, are screaming loudly now. I believe I have everyone's attention. "Stay right there, big boy, or I'll see what color your blood is," I manage to say. Weak, but it's the best I can come up with at the moment. Mt. Rushmore stands perfectly still and sneers at me with a look that says I won't really shoot him. I decide he'll be wrong if he doesn't behave, and it'll be hard to miss someone so big.

I see that Keeker still has her weapon pointed at Ireland, and she instructs me, "Keep your gun on the big fella and shoot if he acts up." I nod my head up and down, making my nose hurt even more. I feel like shooting myself to end my misery. She then says I should put the plastic restraints on Ireland, but I find they're no longer in my back pocket. So she continues to cover Ireland while I point my shaking gun at the giant. I keep my finger away from the trigger so I don't accidentally discharge it, and my captive continues to give me a look promising instantaneous death as soon as he can get to me.

The bartender, dancers, the staff, and the customers are nowhere to be seen. I'm wondering if the big guy is the club's owner or manager. Keeker tells Ireland, the groggy Ms. Goldson, and the huge guy that they need to remain still and be quiet. She then fishes her cell phone out of her pocket and calls the police. I smile as she calmly speaks into the phone and reports, "This is PI Keeker, license number 79665. Please send a squad car to Show Stoppers II on Whittier Boulevard. We have shots fired and a guy wanted by Alabama authorities for suspicion of murder. Please hurry." Then she hangs up.

Ireland starts begging us to let him and his girlfriend go. He looks at me and pleads, "I'll leave you and your family alone, and I'll never bother you again. We have some cash, and you and the lady are welcome to it. Suzy and I just want to leave the country."

I say nothing and keep holding my nose to stem the bleeding. Keeker tells Ireland, "Keep your trap shut!"

He does, but Goldson blurts out, "He made me go with him. I'm innocent." No one bothers to respond to her whiney protest.

The police arrive in about five minutes and break the uncomfortable silence in the club. The big guys immediately starts yelling, "I want all of these people arrested for interfering with the operation of my business!"

A plainclothes cop replies, "Shut up, Bruno. You'll get a chance to give your side of this." The cop in the suit then tells Keeker and me to give him our weapons while the other three are being cuffed. We comply. A patrolman starts to handcuff me, and Keeker says to the suit, "He's my client, Detective Davis. He doesn't need to be restrained." The suit nods at the officer, and he lets me go.

One of the uniformed cops tells Detective Davis that there are three cars outside to transport Bruno, Ireland, and Goldson downtown. He nods, and the three are led away. I notice that Ireland is sobbing, and I feel no mercy for him as I think of him killing Gayle Wade and threatening me and my family. I hope to arrange for him never to see the light of day again, and other than my nose, my plan is working perfectly so far.

CHAPTER 38

FRIDAY

6:00 P.M.

Detective Davis drives Keeker and me to a local hospital where they treat my nose. I hand the intake clerk my insurance ID card, and they ask me for a $50 copayment. *This credit card is getting a workout*, I think. They clean the dried blood out of my nostrils and pack it, which is worse than the dried blood. They tell me to leave the packing in for twenty-four hours, but I make no such promise.

After giving me an ice bag to apply to my nose, I'm released. As soon as I get outside, I take out the packing myself and throw it in a trashcan. I'd prefer to bleed over having my nose stopped up. Keeker hands me some tissues, and I begin dabbing to catch the blood. She smiles at me, but I conclude she is more amused than impressed.

Detective Davis then drives the three of us to the local precinct and takes Keeker and me to an interrogation room.

There, we sit for an hour and a half. There's a pad of paper and some pens lying on a wooden table flanked by four chairs. Keeker writes me a note saying, "Don't talk. They're listening." She then tears the paper into tiny pieces and puts them in her purse. Detective Davis finally shows up.

He says, "Just to let you know, we released Bruno Banet, the club owner. His attorney showed up, and we don't think there are any charges to be made against him unless you disagree."

I told him, "He was about to get involved in our situation by bashing Emily here in the back of the head. That's why I fired into the ceiling so he'd stop."

Davis answers, "Well, he can't be held responsible for what you thought he might do."

I understood where he was coming from and remained silent.

The detective then says, "Ms. Keeker, tell me what you and your friend were doing in the club. I'm all ears."

She responded, "We were trying to run this guy down and get him placed in custody. He's threatened my client and his family. Additionally, he's wanted for questioning for a murder, and my client recently uncovered hard evidence that should cook his goose."

Davis asked what evidence she meant, and I took out the recording I had made from the original recorder I recovered a few days ago. I handed the digital recorder to him, and he hit the Play button and listened to it in its entirety.

When he was finished, Davis said, "You say this is a recording of a murder, and you witnessed it?" I responded in the affirmative, and he asked, "Did you talk to the local police about what you saw?" I told him I hadn't because I didn't want to explain that I was outside of the victim's house with my own gun when Ireland showed up. "I can see how that might make you look bad," he said. "Frankly, it does make you look bad."

At this point, I think I owe the detective full disclosure and ask Keeker if she agrees. She shakes her head yes, and I go through my story for the second time in two days, adding in the events of today. I leave out the part about Keeker putting a GPS tracking device on Goldson's car because I don't know if that might get her in trouble. Thankfully, he didn't ask about how we managed to follow Ireland and Goldson for over two hours.

When I finished, Detective Davis leans back and says, "Ireland says you're after him, and he and his girlfriend were going to ask Bruno for a loan so they could go to Mexico to hide from you two."

I reply, "I was after him but not to kill him. I just need him off of the streets, for a long time hopefully."

The detective adds, "I'm going to make a call to the Birmingham Police to confirm your story. What do you want me to tell them about why you decided to try to grab Ireland yourself?"

I said, "I guess you can say I saw Ireland not being found for several months, and I wanted to get something done. I had to pull out all of the stops when he started talking about my kids. By the way, you still have Ireland here, don't you?"

He looks at me like I'm an idiot and replies, "Yeah."

This time, Detective Davis is gone for forty-five minutes when it occurs to me that it's late evening in Birmingham. I hope he can get in touch with Detective Skirvin. I turn to

Keeker and ask her why she's being so quiet, and she gives me the hush sign with her finger, pointing to the large reflective window. I think to myself it must be one-way glass, and someone could be watching and listening on the other side. I think she's being overly cautious, but I decide to give her the benefit of the doubt and don't ask her anything further.

Finally, Detective Davis comes back into the room and announces, "I reached Detective Skirvin at his home. He confirmed that Ireland is a person of interest in a murder in Helena, Alabama. That's enough for us to hold him for the next forty-eight hours, although we may release the girlfriend. Detective Skirvin also said he had no idea that you, Mr. Harrington, were so involved in this matter, and to be frank, he's pretty upset with you. He would like you to call him the first thing Monday morning. You might want to plan on traveling to the Birmingham area for questioning in the near future."

I looked at the floor and managed, "Got it."

Davis added, "By the way, I told him you apparently have the murderer's voice and the victim's voice on tape leading up to the shooting. He didn't know what to say to that. I didn't tell him that you threw away the murder weapon or weapons so you might be looking at an obstruction of justice charge for that alone."

I thought to myself that if it comes to that, it's preferable to Ireland being on the loose to pose a threat to my kids. I still don't see any better way out of this problem than my present course. It could get even more interesting, I admit to myself.

By 8:30 p.m., Keeker and I are being released—me on my own recognizance and she with no charges filed. I figure the differentiation has something to do with the fact I can still land in legal trouble. But I don't ask and am glad to leave. Before I go, I ask Detective Davis if there is any chance that Ireland can leave the lockup under any circumstance other than in the custody of Alabama law enforcements officials. He answers, "Our right to hold him for forty-eight hours, not counting weekends, is pretty solid. And I believe the Birmingham Police will be interested in collecting him by no later than Monday or Tuesday as long as extradition is waived." That sounds good to me.

CHAPTER 39

As we drive back to San Diego, I ask Keeker if she thinks things turned out pretty well. She answers, "I'm glad we got that scumbag off the street. As far as your well-being from a legal standpoint is concerned, we'll have to wait and see. Your biggest obstacle is probably going to be the disposal of the two guns. Hopefully, the tape will save your skin." I swallow nervously and watch the street signs flash by as Keeker drives like a maniac toward San Diego. I reach up to scratch my nose and receive a jolt of pain for my efforts. I'm anxious to go home tomorrow, and I'm leery of my future. But at least, I tell myself, I shouldn't have to worry about messages being painted on my garage door if there is any publicity this time. Little did I know that there would be more than just a little media attention to this case.

When we get back to Keeker's parking lot, my ego is bruised when she makes no comment or gesture I can interpret as an invitation to spend some time with her this evening of a personal nature. I wasn't prepared to do anything of the sort, but I wanted to believe she at least was attracted to me enough to make an offer. She says she'll calculate her total fees and expenses and send a reimbursement check for what she owes me. I tell her I'm thrilled with how things turned out and not to worry about giving me any money back. She cracks that I might need it for a nose job, and I reply with a laugh, "I didn't think it was noticeable."

When I shake hands good-bye with her, I glance at my face in the reflection of the office's glass door and am shocked. I look like I've been hit in the face with a bag of quarters for an hour and then run through a meat grinder. Man, I wouldn't want to spend any time with me either, and I get in my car to drive back to my hotel.

As soon as I get to the room, I call Delta and move my flight up to tomorrow morning at 10:20 a.m. I'm informed that I have to pay a change fee and the difference between my new flight's fare and the previously reserved one. Accordingly, my credit card gets dinged for another $420. I put some ice in a towel and try to press it against my nose. It helps a little, and I switch on the TV. I surf a little until I find a news channel out of Los Angeles. I start as I recognize the outside of Show Stoppers II being shown on the screen.

I turn up the sound and hear the talking head say, "...and bystanders confirm that at least two shots were fired in the exotic dancing club shortly after four thirty this afternoon. The owner of the strip joint, Bruno Banet, didn't return our phone calls asking for more details. Banet is a well-known local businessman with suspected ties to organized crime. And now the weather forecast..."

Wow, I thought. I fired a gun in a business owned by a connected guy. I hope he doesn't look for me to pay the repair fee for the holes I made in his ceiling. I decide I won't worry about Bruno as I can't come up with any good reason for him to pursue me. I hope I'm right.

I turn off the TV and get ready to hit the sack. I notice I have a voice mail on my cell phone. I listen, and it's from my son. He's thanking for arranging for the room in Hot Springs. He says the area is beautiful, and he's even looking forward to seeing his sister tomorrow. I tear up a little, thinking about how worried I was about my kids over the last few days. I'm glad they're at a resort together, and I wish I could be there with them. I turn over, bump my sore nose, moan, and soon fall asleep.

CHAPTER 40

SATURDAY

When I wake up at 7:30 a.m. local time, I check the mirror and see the swelling on and around my nose has gone down, and the pain has lessened a little. But I'm very black and blue. I shower and shave and put on a clean golf shirt, slacks, and shoes. I get to the airport at 8:45 a.m. and find the Crown Room. I snack on their fare and board the plane at 9:40 a.m. Again, I'm upgraded to first class as a result of my frequent flyer status. My seat neighbor does a double take at my face and asks me if I'm married. I laugh and say I'm only engaged and scared to take things any further. I then go to sleep and only wake up to eat the catered lunch.

The plane lands at 6:15 p.m. local time. The day is nearly all used up traveling, which is what happens when you fly from the West Coast to almost the East Coast. I deplane and pick up my luggage from the red baggage area. I ride a bus to my car and get out of the covered parking garage for a modest number of my frequent parking points. I drive to 85 N and onward to 400 N toward Alpharetta. I'm anxious to get home and relax. I think about going to church tomorrow and seeing Elaine, but I think twice about it because of my busted face. I decide I'll make my mind up in the morning when I see what's staring back at me in the mirror.

I pull into my driveway and am, once more, glad there are no messages on my garage door. I hope there are none on the phone either. After pressing the door opener and parking the car in its usual spot, I realize I forgot to call my dog sitter, Pat. I find her in the living room with my two furry "children." I pay her for her time and tell her I'll let her know sometime tomorrow about my schedule for next week. She asks about my face, and I tell her I ran into something. I don't tell her it was an elbow.

I unpack and get ready for bed. I don't turn on the TV and try not to think about my upcoming conversation with Detective Skirvin on Monday. I'm surprised he doesn't want me in Birmingham tomorrow. I set my alarm for 7:00 a.m. I wasn't gone long enough to have any significant jet lag. I'm out like a light no more than thirty seconds after my head hits the pillow.

CHAPTER 41

SUNDAY

I hit the alarm "kill" button and get up at 7:01 a.m. I feel like I've been hit by a truck. I trudge to the mirror, fearing I'll look like I've been hit by one too. Surprisingly, I look better. Interestingly enough, some of the black and bluish areas near my nose are turning yellow. I decide to go to church and maybe make contact with Elaine. Fortunately, it's my teaching partner's turn to lead the lesson for the Sunday school boys today, and I don't have to be prepared. I can just be his sidekick who looks like he lost a bar fight. I'll need to make up something to tell everyone this morning. I decide to go with the story that I fell while working in the yard. It sounds more believable than I was elbowed in a stripper joint while shooting a gun and helping catch a murderer yesterday.

I park, walk into the church, and immediately see Elaine. My heart beats faster, a lump forms in my throat, and my voice starts to crack before I try to speak. It's business as usual, unfortunately. I manage to say hi to her, and she does a double take when she spots my face. She walks over and asks me what happened. I take a huge leap and ask her if I can tell her about it over lunch. To my delight and trepidation, she says yes. I'm practically speechless and manage to say I'll meet her at the front door at noon. She smiles, my heart melts, and she walks away. My immediate thought is where to take her. I decide to let her decide. What a decision, I think.

I sit through the service and then head over to the youth building to help teach the tenth grade boys. I'm daydreaming about Elaine at the beginning of the class when one of them says, "Mr. Harrington, we're all wondering what happened to you."

I don't think a story about falling will suffice for this group, so I answer, "I talked back to my mother." They laugh heartily, and to my relief, query me no more about the condition of my beak. If only it were as easy with adults.

Shortly after noon, I find Elaine standing by the front door. We walk to my car, and I open the passenger door for her. As she slides into the seat, I think to myself she is beautiful and must be crazy for going anywhere with me. I practically run around the car to get in before she changes her mind and runs for it. I ask her where she wants to go, and she says she doesn't care. I drive her to a steak house with a steeply priced menu. No sense in letting my credit card get any rest, I tell myself.

We order entrees and make small talk. I find myself staring into her eyes and worry that it will make her nervous. She doesn't seem to notice, so I continue to indulge myself. We identify most of the people at church we both know and go over many of their more obvious faults when she leans closer to me and asks, "So what happened to your face? You won't be able to model for a few weeks, I guess."

First, I feel thrilled that she has given me a compliment on my looks, maybe. Then I briefly ponder what to say and surprise myself by basically telling her the truth. I leave out a few of the more scary facts like I fired a gun and may be facing serious legal problems. I rationalize that I have to save something to talk about on the second date. Over the course of the next ninety minutes, I find out that she, and apparently most of the world, are pretty knowledgeable about the fact I was accused of sexual misconduct with a woman in Alabama, who ended up being murdered, several months ago. I'm surprised when she tells me that many of the church members said they thought I was guilty, especially when I missed church for a week or two. Well, I thought to myself, there's the making of another good story to tell her. Maybe on the third date.

I explain that I was in California the last couple of days helping the police to catch the guy who killed the woman in Alabama. She looked at me in amazement as if I'd just grown a third ear. Trying not to make myself sound like James Bond, I briefly tell her about hiring the investigative company to get a lead on Ireland's whereabouts and then enlisting the services of Emily Keeker. I conclude with the apprehension in the strip club, the friendly conversation in the police station, and my pending appointment to talk with the Birmingham Police tomorrow.

When I finish, I sense that she thinks I'm some kind of liar with visions of grandeur. Instead, she remarks, "It's a wonder you don't look even worse, considering how you spend your weekends." I experience a flood of relief and laugh with her. I'm thinking that she actually doesn't know the half of it, which in fact she doesn't. I tell myself there will hopefully be time for full disclosure later.

I look around and determine that we've apparently outlasted everyone who was in the restaurant when we arrived. I take her back to her car in the church parking lot and give her a hug good-bye. I decide I really like hugging her. I promise to call her in the next few days while telling myself I hope I can deliver on it. I drive home in a good mood despite my pending meeting with Detective Skirvin. I tell myself that at least my next big crisis isn't until tomorrow. I'll soon find out that I'm wrong on this count.

I get home at about 4:00 p.m. and turn on the Braves game. They're playing a tight game with the Phillies. I walk into the kitchen to get something to drink when I see the phone screen with information on it. Noting that I don't have a message waiting, I check the call log and see a number starting with 213. The caller ID stuns me because it says, *Los Angeles Times*. I panic for a moment and wonder if I should call Detective Skirvin, but what can he do about it? I have an uneasy premonition and turn the channel to CNN. After a few minutes, I know why *the Times* called me. The story has apparently gone nationwide and, likely, viral.

I recognize the Show Stoppers II from a live helicopter feed while the male newscaster says, "You're looking at Show Stoppers II, an adult exotic dancing club, referred to by most as a strip club. It's owned by Bruno Banet, a local man known to have underworld connections. We've learned from confidential sources that a man wanted for questioning in connection with a murder in Alabama was detained in the club yesterday until police arrived to take custody of him. This appears to be very close to a so-called citizen's arrest in that a Georgia man, Kevin Harrington, apparently tracked down Bob Ireland of Birmingham and helped detain him until police arrived. A source close to the incident told CNN that Harrington tracked Ireland to San Diego with the help of Hearty Investigations, a Nashville, Tennessee firm. He then secured the services of Emily Keeker, a San Diego private investigator. Apparently, Keeker and Harrington followed Ireland and his stripper girlfriend, Peggy Goldson of San Diego, to the LA club and managed to detain Ireland until the police arrived. Two gunshots were said to be fired into the ceiling by Harrington during a scuffle. A source close to the precinct holding Ireland told CNN that the suspect is awaiting extradition to the Birmingham, Alabama, police department that is handling the murder case. We'll bring you more on this story as it develops."

Well, I think to myself, more details are getting out from somewhere. I pick up my cell phone and call Keeker, who answers on the first ring. "Emily, you know who's spilling the beans to the news media?"

She answers, "There are several leaks in the police department, and I also talked to CNN a few hours ago."

I was surprised and asked, "Why?"

She replied, "Are you kidding? It's great for my rep, and the story will probably get me more business." I see no reason to ask her to stay quiet since she likes the publicity. I tell her good-bye and hang up.

I decide I'm not talking to anyone in the media for right now. I also wonder how my weekend adventure might affect my job status. I think I'll probably need to call the Disability Protection Group legal department tomorrow right after I talk with Detective Skirvin. And a call to Elaine may be in order, although I've already given her the basics of what happened. Wonder what she'll think about me being a "gunman." Things seem to be getting a little complicated again. I unplug the home phone line and try to have a quiet Sunday evening. I turn off the TV and try reading for a little while. I give up and go to bed at 9:00 p.m.

CHAPTER 42

MONDAY

It's no surprise to me that the Atlanta paper runs a story on Ireland's capture and my involvement. A small caption indicates it's a reprint of an article that ran yesterday in the *Los Angeles Times*. I feel like I may need a publicist if things don't settle down. I get cleaned up at about 8:00 a.m. after jogging two miles. A couple of early-rising neighbors are out in their yards, puttering around. They wave at me as I run by their houses. *Great*, I think, *now I'm becoming a reluctant celebrity.*

At 9:00 a.m.—8:00 a.m. in Birmingham—I call Detective Skirvin. He tells me what I expect to hear, "How fast can you get here?" I tell him I can be there between 11:30 a.m. and noon. He gives me the street address of the department and hangs up without saying good-bye. I can't blame him for being short with me.

Since my activities are becoming well-chronicled, I call my boss. He answers the call, "This is Doug Wills. How may I help you?" I tell him I need to take today as a vacation day. To his credit, he doesn't ask why. I say I intend to keep my appointments for the rest of the week on Tuesday, Wednesday, and Thursday. I'm scheduled to fly to Shreveport, Louisiana tomorrow and return the following night.

I almost decide to not call Buster Todd of the DPG legal department, but I do so to keep it from seeming as if I'm trying to hide something from him. I reach him, and he tells me he's already heard from the Birmingham attorney who assisted me, in a manner of speaking, Mr. Patterson. Todd says Patterson's been in touch with Detective Skirvin, and he caught me on the news. "You've been kind of busy, haven't you?" asks Todd. I reply that I'm taking care of my family and myself as best I can, and he shouldn't believe everything he sees on TV or reads in the newspaper. I swallow as I think to myself everything I've seen on TV or read in the paper has, in fact, been true.

I tell Todd I want him to know I'm taking a vacation day and going to Birmingham to talk with Detective Skirvin. He thanks me, adding that Patterson has already told him of my appointment. I emphasize that I plan to be back on the job doing my usual duties tomorrow. I breathe a sigh of relief when Todd says nothing further. I figure my job status must be okay at the moment. I shudder when I consider that perhaps the admission of disposing of a murder weapon might change all that. I let my dogs outside and call Pat to come over and let them out later today. She agrees to do this for me, and I leave. I figure I can call Elaine briefly on the way.

I dial Elaine, and she doesn't answer. I leave her a message and tell her I'll call her in a day or two. I add that my recent adventure is apparently getting more media attention, which she'll likely notice. I get a phone call from Hot Springs, Arkansas, from my kids. They are amazed about what they've seen on TV about me. I tell them I'll explain it in detail, but I'm on the way to talk to the Birmingham police right now. After saying good-bye, I realize I should call my mother in case she's heard any of the media reports. I place the call, and mom tells me she hasn't heard a thing recently about me or the murdered Alabama woman who lied about me. I figure her TV stays locked on *Let's Make A Deal* and soap operas. I tell her that I'm in the news again because I assisted in catching the guy who killed the woman who accused me of assaulting her. She hesitates and says, "Good." I have the feeling that she isn't fully processing this information, and I promise to call her and talk things out in a few days.

Just before 11:30 a.m., I pull up to the main office of the Birmingham Police Department. I go to the front desk and tell the clerk I'm here to see Detective Skirvin. In a few minutes, I'm ushered to a conference room. Detective Skirvin and an associate come in about fifteen minutes later. He is angry.

"Harrington, I can't believe you didn't bring an attorney with you. I should arrest you for obstruction of justice," he says loudly. "You disposed of two guns, one or both of which was a murder weapon. Also, you were an eyewitness in an active murder case and didn't come forward," he adds. "And best of all," he continues, "you had an audio tape of the murder and kept that a secret to yourself." He stands and walks to the end of the table, right next to me before shouting, "I can throw the book at you!"

I reply in as strong a tone I can muster, "I only recovered the tape a few days ago. I can show you where I dumped the guns, and I can explain what I did and why I did it, although it won't justify my actions."

The detective looks at me, smirks, and says, "I just bet you can, and no, I'm betting it won't."

I then proceed to tell my entire story to Detective Skirvin, leaving out nothing. I emphasize that I have no excuse for my secret trip to Wade's house on that Sunday night other than I was under incredible stress and at the end of my rope. I explain that I, thankfully, came to my senses and was preparing to leave until I saw Ireland arrive. I add that part of the reason I was keeping things to myself was I didn't know the Birmingham police were skeptical of Wade's and Ireland's story. Plus, I tell him I was hoping Ireland would leave me alone if I didn't talk, but I know now that he viewed me as a loose end.

When I finished, the detective sits still and stares at the wall behind me for what seems like forever. I say nothing to break the uncomfortable silence, which goes on for five minutes. He then gives me an exasperated look and grunts, "Wait here. I'll be right back." He returns quickly with a manila folder and opens it on the table. "Mr. Harrington," he says, "you are one of the luckiest guys I've ever met. In fact, it's a wonder you're not dead. Detective Davis of LAPD is apparently very good at his job and convinced Mr. Ireland that he has no advantage in fighting extradition to Alabama. I believe he used the existence of your tape to convince him of the futility in remaining a guest at their jail since it would only be a matter of time before we would bring him back here. I'm told he has officially waived extradition. Detective Davis also reported Ireland's already called his Birmingham attorney, Matt Geary, and wants him to represent him when he returns.

"I'm flying out there personally tomorrow to pick him up. I'm not giving you any promises that we won't bring charges against you in the future, and if you fail to cooperate with us in any way from now on, I promise we will come after you. That being said, I'm going to present you with three requests, but they're really more like orders. If you work with us in all three areas, you might not need an attorney to represent you in this matter."

I nod my head and think to myself, *Maybe I should've brought a lawyer with me.*

Detective Skirvin resumes, "First, we'll need you to testify in court against Ireland after we charge him and try him for the murder of Gayle Wade. Second, I'll need the original digital recorder with the taping of the shooting on it. And third, you'll lead two of my officers to the spot where you tossed Ireland's gun and your gun into the Cahaba River. You have a problem with any of this?"

I shake my head from side to side and reply, "No, sir, I have no problem with anything you just said."

Detective Skirvin then tells me, "Then you and I have a verbal agreement, and remember, if you do anything to piss me off before Ireland is tried and convicted, I'll come after you with the full force of the law. Consider yourself to be on personal probation with me, mister." I again agree to cooperate with him, and he tells me to wait in the room until he finds a couple of guys to follow me down the interstate to the bridge where I dumped the guns.

I wait for a couple of young policemen who then follow me in an unmarked car. When I reach the Cahaba River bridge on the interstate, I show them exactly where I tossed the guns over the edge. They tell me good-bye, and I leave them on the roadside with their blue lights flashing while they talk on their cell phones. I can't decide if I want the guns to be found or not.

I arrive back home at 5:30 p.m. I go to my home office upstairs and begin preparing for my trip to Louisiana in the morning. At 11:00 p.m., I put my dogs on leashes and let them use the bathroom in the front yard. For the life of me, I can't figure out why it's a treat for them to go on leashes in the front yard instead of being on their own in the backyard.

CHAPTER 43

FRIDAY (FOUR DAYS LATER)

I'm working at home today. I have three field visits to dictate and a few calls to make to firm up next week's schedule. I reconnected my home phone to the wall jack when I returned from Birmingham on Monday and have received several messages from different media sources asking me for an interview or for my comments on the capture of Ireland. I listened to several when I returned home last night from an assignment in Tennessee. Interestingly enough, none of the claimants I've interviewed have acted like they know who I am or what's happened to me.

Tomorrow, I'm looking forward to having the steel reinforced door removed from my bedroom entrance. It clashes with my bedroom décor, and I want my original door reinstalled. I feel good about getting rid of a symbol of my insecurity when I wasn't safe in my own house or anywhere else. I also call my security company and change my top-of-the-line home security plan with cameras and direct police notification back to the normal program in which an alarm sounds if a door or window is compromised. With Ireland on ice, I don't need to be set up like Fort Knox. I hope to be able to sell the steel door on Craig's List.

Shortly after 3:00 p.m., I answer the phone, and it's a male claiming to represent *Good Morning America*, the national news program. He tells me that their surveys indicate that a large number of viewers are interested in seeing the Georgia Bounty Hunter on the show. I didn't know this was the term being used to refer to me, and I wonder if this guy made it up just now. I ask if there is a fee paid to guests, and he tells me that my travel expenses are reimbursed, but *GMA* considers it inappropriate to pay its guests appearance fees.

I take his name and number and tell him I'll call him back. I think about this and decide it might be an excellent way to finally clear my name with respect to any lingering damage to my reputation from the original sexual assault accusation. I call him back at 3:45 p.m. and tell him I'll do it. We decide on a week from today, and he confirms my address and e-mail address, as well as the spelling of my name, my date of birth, and Social Security number.

He advises I'll receive a round-trip airline ticket for Atlanta to New York City for next Thursday and Friday. He adds that my hotel accommodations will be included in the overnight package, and I'll have limo service to the show and then to the airport for my return flight. He asks that I not discuss my appearance with anyone, even after the show starts to promote it next week. I assure him I'll keep it quiet, but I know I'll tell

Elaine about it. I admit to myself that I want to impress her and figure it'll be great to see her reaction during our date tomorrow night. I briefly think about calling Buster Todd but this is actually a personal choice, and the show is going to be about the capture of Ireland in Los Angeles. Since my job is not going to be discussed—I hope—I decide I'm only required to use vacation days to cover next Thursday and Friday, and I have plenty of those.

CHAPTER 44

FRIDAY: A WEEK LATER

It's 5:00 a.m., and I'm riding in a chauffeur-driven limousine to the Good Morning America studio in Times Square. I see a lot of people on the streets even though it's early. I arrive and am dropped off at the front entrance with a big ABC logo over the door. I'm met by a guy waiting at the door, who hits an electronic lock and admits me to the lobby. He escorts me to a conference room, not unlike the one in which Detective Skirvin and me had our recent heartwarming talk.

I'm shown where the bathroom is and asked if I want a cup of coffee and a doughnut. I say yes to the doughnut but ask for a Coke to drink. The food is delivered by a young man a short time later, along with a copy of the New York Times. There is also a TV playing a local ABC channel, but the volume is extremely low. Just before 6:30 a.m., one of the show's hosts, Robin Roberts, walks into the room and introduces herself to me. I'm impressed with how friendly she is and her ability to make me feel comfortable so quickly. She tells me I'm scheduled to be on the set at 7:26 a.m. and will be on air with her for something between 2–4 minutes. She advises me to try to relax, keep my mind blank, respond to her questions in a clear, steady voice and avoid giving too much detail. She then shakes my hand again and is rushed out of the room by a studio worker.

I'm getting real nervous and tell myself that I have to pretend I'm talking to Robin in my family room at home. I decide I'll look directly at her and try to ignore the cameras. A makeup person comes into the room and applies cosmetics to my face a little after 7:00 a.m. At 7:15 a.m., the same guy who brought me the Coke and doughnut leads me to an interview area and seats me in a wingback chair. It's hard and has a straight back. Robin isn't in the room yet, but there are two manned cameras and a guy on a PC. At about 7:20 a.m., a guy enters the room and says he is one of the show's producers. He thanks me for coming and asks me if I'm nervous. I respond in the affirmative. He tells me to breathe deeply and to concentrate on Robin as if I'm having a one on one conversation with her. I tell him I'll do my best, and he pats me on the shoulder and says I'll be fine.

A few minutes later, Robin walks in and smiles at me. She takes a seat across from me, and I hear a countdown begin. "Five, four, three, two, one."

Robin then says, "We have a guest today who has drawn national attention because of his incredible capture of a murder suspect in Los Angeles the week before last. We have Kevin Harrington in studio today. Welcome, Kevin."

She looks at me, and I take a deep breath and reply, "Thanks, Robin." I think to myself, *There, that wasn't too much detail.*

Robin then continues, "Kevin was falsely accused of sexual assault by a woman in Alabama several months ago, a Ms. Gayle Wade. She and an accomplice, Bob Ireland, basically conspired to make a false claim of assault in order to extort money from Kevin's employer, Disability Protection Group. In a bizarre twist, Ireland murdered Wade and tried to frame Kevin for the killing."

She hesitates briefly while the audience gasps. She resumes, "But Kevin here was an eyewitness to the shooting, and despite searching for several months, the police couldn't find Ireland. Then Kevin did the police department's work for them. Tell our audience how you managed to find and apprehend a killer that was successfully eluding the police, Kevin."

I clam up for a few seconds and try to gather myself before replying, "Well, Robin, first, I'd like to say that the Birmingham, Alabama, police have done great work in the case, particularly Detective Dave Skirvin. Without his tireless efforts, I wouldn't be safe from Ireland today."

I pause briefly, and it occurs to me that I won't look too good if I discuss stalking around outside Wade's house or dumping a murder weapon. Before I can resume, Robin interjects, "Yes, Kevin but you were responsible for taking action that not only led to the suspect being located but you were personally involved in catching him. Tell us about how that happened please."

I think to myself, *Thanks, Robin. Now I can skip the uncomfortable stuff.*

I straighten up in my chair and explain, "Well, I was worried about my safety and the safety of my loved ones since a murderer with a grudge against me was on the loose. I contacted an investigation company, Hearty Investigative, and they began canvassing friends and relatives of Ireland. They were able to talk with a cousin of Ireland in the Birmingham area who gave them a post office box address he was using in San Diego. I then hired a private investigator recommended by Hearty, Ms. Emily Keeker. By the way, she is a great PI. We spotted Ireland picking up some mail and were able to determine where he was staying."

Robin says, "He was living with an exotic dancer, isn't that right?"

I respond, "That's right. We ended up following Ireland and his girlfriend to a strip club in Los Angeles that is connected to the club that employed her in San Diego."

Robin asks me, "And then you and the PI, Keeker, apprehended Ireland, isn't that right?"

"Yes," I say.

Robin counters, "Why didn't you call the local police to pick him up?"

I respond, "Well, Robin, we had him in the club right then, and I was worried he would go off the grid again if he got away. My partner was armed, and we decided to secure Ireland and then call the police."

A smattering of applause breaks out in the audience. Robin smiles and says, "Yes, this is a brave man, don't you agree?" Then a general round of audience clapping takes place, and I'm sure I blush nicely for the cameras.

Robin looks at me and says, "Kevin, you work for a disability carrier and interview people. Yet I'm told you had to fire two shots during the capture. Can you tell us about that?"

I say, "I was given a gun by Keeker in the event things didn't go well. At one point, the club owner—"

Robin interjects, "Bruno Banet, a guy with underworld connections."

I continue, "Yes, that's right. He was coming up behind Keeker with a blackjack or something. I fired two shots into the ceiling, hoping it would stop him or at least slow him down. Thankfully, it worked."

Robin then remarks, "Well, I'm sure the audience will agree with me that you are apparently a resourceful and brave man."

Again, there is a round of applause. She then concludes by saying, "*GMA* would like to thank Kevin Harrington for being on the show today. The suspect he apprehended is now jailed in Birmingham and awaiting trial for the murder of Gayle Wade. Let's have a big round of applause for the Georgia Bounty Hunter, Kevin Harrington." There is more clapping and some cheers before Robin asks one final question, "Any chance you might go into the bounty hunting business?"

I smile and say, "No, I work for a great company and enjoy being a field representative."

Robin smiles at me and the camera and says, "It's time for a break, and we'll have a look at today's weather when we come back."

I'm relieved the piece is over and even more relieved that I didn't get pushed into discussing anything that would've been hard to explain, like stalking a woman at night and dumping a murder weapon. Robin shakes my hand, hugs me, and wishes me well. I thank her and follow the same guy who earlier brought me food. He leads me out of the studio and onto a crowded Times Square street. There is a limo waiting, and I get in for a 45-minute ride to the airport. I'm sweaty and tired, making it easy to sleep on the flight home.

CHAPTER 45

FRIDAY: THREE WEEKS LATER

I was a celebrity for a few days and received several congratulatory calls from friends, coworkers and relatives. Another good thing is that the requests for interviews and other guest appearances stopped. I guess no one is interested in old news. My life is starting to come back together nicely. Detective Skirvin seems to be in a better mood with me now; maybe complimenting him on national TV helped. He advised me recently that the trial for Ireland will probably not take place until next year. That's okay, as I'm in no hurry to give a deposition and, eventually, testify. I also receive a warm call from Keeker, who thanks me for mentioning her name on *GMA* and her role in the capture so prominently. I tell her I was just telling the truth, and she said to look her up the next time I'm on the West Coast. Not much chance of that happening, I think.

My job is going well, and since I've not heard from Buster Todd, I assume I'm not in any kind of hot water. The vice president of the claim area called me on my cell phone last week and congratulated me for the way things worked out. My relationship with Elaine is progressing nicely but slowly, which is fine. We see each other once or twice a week not counting at church on Sundays.

It's Friday night, and I'm arriving home after dropping off Elaine. I fall asleep watching the news and wake up at 12:45 a.m. Again, my dogs want to relieve themselves in the front yard and both of them whine and stand by the front door. I attach their leashes and take them out. I yawn while they do their business. I look forward to a normal Saturday of jogging, lawn care activities, and attending a cookout at my neighbor's house in the afternoon. I bring the dogs in, switch off the porch light, and head for bed.

ONE BLOCK AWAY

The car with Alabama plates has a clear line of sight to the Harrington house. The man behind the wheel thinks about his cousin Bob rotting in jail, waiting to be tried for killing that worthless lying excuse for a woman. He takes another drag from his cigarette and puts it out in the ashtray. He just finished watching his target walk out of the front door of his house with his two dogs and stand for a few minutes in the yard while they did their business. The target is now back inside his home, and the lights upstairs went out a short time ago. The man thinks he should probably wait a little longer, but he's anxious to avenge his cousin, the best and only friend he ever had. He practically smolders thinking about watching this clown on *Good Morning America* trashing Bob. He feels ashamed that he gave up Bob's mailing address. He hits the kill switch to prevent the car's interior lights from coming on when he opens the door. He checks the magazine of his gun and reinserts it into the handle. He checks the silencer. It's one Bob actually gave him. He puts the gun back in his jacket pocket. He then opens the car door quietly, smiles, and starts down the street toward the target's house.